Remember when you were little?

Remember when there were monsters under your bed and unseen things lived in your closet? You heard them at night, even if nobody else did. Remember when everyone you loved—your mom and dad, your grandfather, the impossible crush who sat across the class from you, your dog—was going to last forever and never die?

Remember birthdays? Remember when every Christmas was an eternity away, and every day was a perfect surprise when you walked out the front door? It was all beautiful and terrifying, in ways that it hasn't been for a long time.

Remember magic? They told you love can't last forever and monsters aren't real. You believed them and you based everything on it, so you let your world go black-and-white.
Come back.

Love letters to all of us, from all of us—the things we remember and the things we've lost.

About *Dear Ghost*

"Trust me, though, when I tell you how I relished every sentence, and how it made me feel both deeply sad and also full of wonder, how perfectly drawn every character was, even the one we never quite meet, and in short, what a beautiful little book this is."

(Lauren Davis, author of *Even So*)

"...one of the most beautiful books I've ever read. A classic."

(Sasha Lauren, author of *The Paris Predicament*)

"There are elements here that evoke Kerouac's *On The Road*, with ideas of travel or the fluidity of place (as places exist more so in our minds than in reality, perhaps), or William Burroughs' *My Education: A Book of Dreams*, as some of Bickford's epistles treat dreams as a deeper truth, more valid than anything which we experience when 'awake.' But Bickford seems less...pretentious, less interested in making a larger 'statement' than simply sharing with us, as though these dispatches are sent out into the world for us, and not Ghost."

(Bart Gazzola, Curated Magazine)

"Bickford writes from a place deep inside that many, unfortunately, refuse to go. What a gift that he does...his humanity, his humanness, touches us all."

(Claudia Piepenburg, author of *Letting Go*)

Love, Ghost

letters from Sunset & Vine

Bob Bickford

Love, Ghost: Letters from Sunset & Vine © 2022 Bob Bickford

ISBN: 978-1-950292-09-7

This book is both fiction and memoir. The characters, incidents and dialogues in this book are products of the author's memory and imagination.

No part of this book may be reproduced or transmitted in any form or by any means, electronic or mechanical, including photocopying, recording, or by any means of information storage and retrieval systems, without permission in writing from the publisher.

Paranormalice Press, LLC
www.paranormalice.com
paranormalicepress@gmail.com
Cover Art by Chris Holmes
Photos credit to Donnez Cardoza
Produced in the U.S.A

For you.

Sometimes the past is just gone. People say it's better that way. Let the dead rest.

The ghosts say different. They gather round in the dark, strangely beautiful, to touch me with hands like butterflies. They sigh and insist they will never leave—that forever is always.

Love, Ghost

D_{ear} Ghost,

You put a hand on my arm. "I'm leaving. Maybe only for a little while."
You stayed very still, watching me. Behind you, the sun touched the ocean. Day turns to night fast, on the sand. The beaches were emptying. Down the strand, the sparkle of water would soon get replaced by bulbs on the Ferris wheel. You shifted the bag strap on your shoulder.
"I played so long," you said. "I need to rest."
The noise of the boulevard went away, leaving only hush, only your face. You never wore perfume. I smelled your fragrances: cotton, suntan oil, oranges, and clean perspiration.
"Will you come back?" I asked.
Neither of us said anything else for a little while.
"If I can find my way, I will," you finally answered. "I'll remember to trail crumbs behind me."
The pain came, then. All the things I ever wanted to say to you ran away. I couldn't speak.
The twilight painted us blue. Hotel and restaurant signs lit up, colored rocks in a river of headlights. It was how I mostly remembered it later, the other colors mixed into all that blue. There must have been the smells of a dry summer—plumeria, vanilla, cigars, warm pavement, with ocean salt beneath all of it. There must have been the sounds of car horns, a small plane overhead.
I don't remember any of it. I only see the watercolor evening.
I only see blue. I only see you.
You come back in colors. My toothbrush is your favorite shade of green. There's a single orange on the kitchen counter. I try to keep at least one there, because you always scolded me for putting fruit in the refrigerator so it's

a way of talking to you. The red and yellow flowers you planted in the front yard glow in the dusk.

    I write you letters, sometimes. I smell ghosts of clean cotton and oranges on the paper. I hear you laugh.
    You thought I was tough enough to get by, but you wouldn't leave the dogs. Not all the way and not for good, so when the windows get dark, I haul myself up from the chair. Sleeping heads lift from paws, instantly alert. I don't know how they know when the leashes are coming out, but they do. They ignore the sidewalk and pull me across grass. I nod to other dog-walkers as we pass. You could never remember people's names, Ghost, but you knew the name of every dog in the neighborhood.
    We walk down to that same corner, the dogs and I. If you're ever there waiting for us, they'll see you even if you're invisible, and no leashes will hold them. No leash will hold me, either.
    Not tonight, though. We watch the traffic for a little while before we turn for home.

Bob Bickford

Love, Ghost

Dear Ghost,

I get tired earlier in the evenings, now.
That's the gentle part about getting old. The yawns creep up, the kind that shudder and creak the corners of my jaw, the kind that take me back to being little. Brush teeth, spit aqua-colored Crest, hand cupped under the faucet. Tap water tastes like clean-nothing these days. I miss the metal taste from the bathroom faucet—it always echoed summer nights, a reminisce about garden hoses.
There's nothing on earth beats a day that makes me squint, green grass, and a mouthful of July water from the hose. The spigot is painted red and it spin-squeaks open, one-two-three twists. Wait while the water runs, first hot from the sun and then suddenly ice cold. Heaven splashes my face wet, my mouth awkward as a first kiss, water spilling past onto the lawn, more goodness than I can take in.
The grass is soaked, spongy cool beneath bare feet, reflecting blue, enough loveliness for the whole world. If I left here with no more than the taste of hose water in my mouth, it would be enough.
Clock says eight. Outside the window, the sky deepens but hangs onto blue until the last second before dark. July is so perfect the blue doesn't want to go.
Good-nights, and my mom curled reading a book, her bare feet tucked beneath her. Her eyes follow me out of the room. My dad lifts his glass in my direction without looking away from the tv, a toast he isn't aware of making.
The light from the hallway falls across the floor to my bed, a sidewalk to the moon. An electric fan swivels back-and-forth, back-and-forth, in front of the open window. A

cloud of moths moves across the streetlight on the corner. The night outside hums with its own business, sweet living creatures I never see during the day.

Nighttime is when the gentle things come out. The dark is where they're safe.

The sheets are blessed cool, a little rough from drying on the line. The clean smell says my mom loves me even if I'm too old to kiss, and summer will never end. I can put my feet on the pillow to steal a little reading from the hall light, but I'm too tired. The fan rattles as it blows breezes from faraway across my forehead and cheeks.

My pillow and drifting—there are planes to fly, bikes to race, bat-crack singles to line over the second baseman's glove. Mostly, there's the little girl who sits at the front of the class to rescue from dragons and fires, bank robbers and rushing locomotives, all sorts of peril and trouble and upset. I started wearing glasses in grade two, but I never need them when I save her. I don't wear them in dreams.

Dreams now, staring into the dark, to take me into dreams.

When I'm gone from here, the moths will still swirl in the streetlight and the gentle creatures beyond the window will go on about their lives. Downstairs, my mom will still turn soft pages and the ice cubes in my dad's drink will chime when he sets down his glass. A two-tone Impala will coast to the curb outside, dropping off the young woman who lives across the street. She's too old to rescue from bank robbers, but she always shows me a sweet smile and a wave. I hope her dreams come true.

You were my best dream, Ghost. The others were practice. I didn't save you from all your dragons, and I didn't always get there in time when you needed help. I'm sorry about that, but you were pretty good at fighting dragons by yourself. Sometimes, you just let me think I helped. You were always kind.

Love, Ghost

In the end, I think we saved each other. That stands, and it's probably enough.

Yawns are nothing to be afraid of, you whisper. Taste the water.

Sweet dreams.

Bob Bickford

Love, Ghost

Dear Ghost,

My parents went on their honeymoon sometime after my first birthday. They married on impulse, like a blurt, so they had to save for the trip. My mom lined up an older woman to stay with me. Mary Poppins was still a couple years from the theaters, but no doubt my mom read the book. She lingered close enough to her own teen years not to trust anyone young, and probably felt sure a dour, umbrella-carrying matron would give me a teaspoon of sugar water in time and be much less likely to invite her boyfriend over.

The honeymooners kissed me goodbye, waved to Poppins, flew on a Constellation propeller plane from Los Angeles to New York, then floated the rest of the way to Europe on the Queen Mary.

My mom had been a rich debutante before she decided to be poor, used to nice things and perfect manners and being lonely, but she had never been to Europe. My dad was older than her, a tough guy, a slum rat, but he had seen France and Germany through the periscope of a Sherman tank. In the ocean liner dining room, he likely watched her because she knew which spoon to eat dessert with. She watched him too, as he spread a map across the hood of their rented Volkswagen in Baden-Württemberg. He knew which mountains came next.

They probably saw each other with different eyes. Maybe it made a good enough reason to fall in love, at least for a little while.

I've seen the color photographs they brought back. There are none of my dad because he needed all the film for her. I see the softness in her eyes, looking out from Europe and only seeing him.

She was prettier than the elegant Parisienne women. She spoke nearly perfect private school French, so felt appalled and hurt because people pretended not to understand her. He made better spaghetti sauce than anyone in Rome, and he knew it. The Italians loved him for reciting his recipe to them, in his Boston accent and using a copy of Berlitz.

They ate lunches in the Beetle back seat from picnic baskets filled with peaches, bread, and cheese, to save money. They drank wine at sidewalk tables, mugged the Little Mermaid, collected pebbles from the beach at Nice, bought tobacco from the shops in Amsterdam, drifted beneath the old bridges in Venice. My mom rarely talked about those places later, perhaps because frequent recall of something splendid risks the magic.

In the end, forming a single perfect memory and finding a way back to it forever might be our whole point. It might be enough.

My parents went to Shangri-la, just that once. I don't know if they're together now. Maybe they had enough of each other when they were here, but if they've stayed constant, I know where to find them. They walk in the early summer of 1962, through a warm, colored rain, somewhere near Paris.

He keeps stopping her so he can take another picture.

Eventually, the Queen Mary returned from across the ocean, bringing my mom and dad back with her. They disembarked and flew west, from New York City to Los Angeles, back to the Hollywood smog and their real lives. I wonder now about their sadness during that voyage. My mom had a box of colored glassware from Venice and a jar full of pebbles from Nice. My dad had his yellow Kodak boxes.

Some things happen only once, and then never again.

My mom told me the homecoming story when I was a teenager. She gave it to me reluctantly, like birthright.

Love, Ghost

They went to find me, straight from the airport. Poppins met them at her front door. The older woman opened up, cordial, wanted to know all about the trip. My still-new mother, who had spent the previous weeks suppressing the idea that a trip away from such a small baby had been unforgivable, had no time for small talk. She tried to stay polite for a minute or two, then gave up.

"Where's Bobby?" she demanded.

The woman seemed startled, like she had forgotten there a baby starred in the play. "He's in the bath—I just put him in when I heard you at the door."

The two women stared at each other, the absent-minded rushing to answer the doorbell flowering into something awful. I can only imagine the horror that passed between them. My mom pushed Poppins aside and sprinted through the house to the bathroom. Unattended, I had slipped beneath the surface. The bathwater lay smooth as a dream, undisturbed by even a ripple.

My mom told me, that teenaged evening years later, that she had never stopped seeing my eyes, looking up at her from the bottom of the tub, or forgotten the single bubble that escaped my lips. She relived those things when she fell asleep at night.

"You smiled underwater," she said. "Like you were glad to see me."

"I didn't drown," I reminded her. "I'm still here."

"You're still here," she echoed. She looked doubtful.

Somehow, I had coughed up water and been okay. Her eyes said I had drowned, nonetheless. Some things happen once but never again, and are better not spoken of, ever again.

It was an accident, but I wasn't done with accidents. Crawling later that year, I pulled a hot percolator by its cord from the coffee table. A half-gallon of scalding liquid dumped over my back and sent me to the hospital. Later in toddlerhood, a boy named Gubber crowned me with a twenty-ounce hammer his dad had left out. He missed becoming a three-year-old murderer by a quarter-inch. I have a white half-moon nested in the hair that grows above my right temple. One afternoon, a swing set upended and caught my arm as it tipped over. I remember arterial blood, warm and bright. I still show scars from wrist to elbow where the doctor stitched me up.

For a while, I seemed determined to finish drowning.

Eventually, the accidents stopped, but the pull of water never left.

My mom was small and fierce, turned into steel by abandonment and disappointment. Weakness terrified her. It reminded her that while she might be small and fierce, the world stayed huge and could be cruel. When I was little, she didn't like my terror at swimming lessons. She didn't like to see me standing on the deck, waiting to dive, shaking from more than cold.

Put your shoulders back, she told me. I'm embarrassed to sit with the other mothers. This isn't how we act.

When I got older, something snapped. Something not entirely good happened. I gave up and fell in love with the water. I found my sweetness in black and cold, my release in unseen currents. Fear became addiction, I turned passionate about swimming, learned to love the smell of chlorine, turned into a pool rat, became an unlikely lifeguard. My mom told me later, when I wore an Adidas jacket covered in swimming patches, that she understood my childish fear. My phobia had been well-born. She had seen my last bubble rise toward her and break on the surface, after all.

I don't know if she understood when she watched me leave a three-meter board, saw me lounged in a lifeguard chair, that it wasn't a triumph over terror, but an armistice, a walking on the very edge. Her own worst fears laughed and danced with mine.

Love, Ghost

I've watched a rip tide tear away the beach on Long Island, my sandy toes inches from the edge. An ocean whirlpool appeared once in South Carolina and sucked a boogie board from beneath me, into the noisy black. I never found it. I have stood beside the Niagara River, rushing past like a locomotive, blue-and-green-and-white before the plunge, with the barest of iron railings between me and the tumult. I've held onto the mast of a swamped catamaran, out of sight of shore, while a summer storm turned a great lake into a boiling cauldron.

"I remember that," you whisper. "Lake Michigan is *big*."

I've felt the attraction of water, resisted the fascination, but I haven't drowned again. Not yet.

I still live with my fear by diving deep. It's my turn to brush past Poppins and run down the hall. I manage invisible currents by swimming with them, dissolving into liquid. I drink cold water and dream about your laugh, Ghost. I smell your skin and see your bubbles rising toward me. I give in to the currents every day and hope they carry me away, back to you.

Some things happen only once, and then never again.

Love, Ghost

Dear Ghost,

    I'm going to tell you a story, which makes me happy, because it's the most complete thing I can give you for now.
    In 1964, we lived in Hollywood.
    I have a million clear memories of the year there. We moved to Kansas in the spring of 1965, when I had just turned four, so the plethora of memories are from when I was three.
    I want you to have a sense of how I remember three.
    Our house was a Craftsman, because it was Hollywood, the west side of Loma Linda Avenue across from the Trianon Apartments. It stayed dark inside, because two very old black walnut trees in the front yard threw perpetual shade. What they dropped on the ground got mushy, moldy, and smelled. I've never cared for walnuts—that's probably why.
    We lived next door to a movie star named Jack Sheldon. I don't know if he was really a movie star, but we thought of him that way. Merv Griffin's sidekick, he played the trumpet solo on "The Shadow of Your Smile". If this was a story, that would be foreshadowing. My mother worried about some of the parties around the Sheldon's back-yard pool. You know the way those movie people are.
    The Goodyear blimp floated by my bedroom window at night, covered in colored lights, terrifying and beautiful all at once. Like you.
    My dad liked it. He sat on my bed sometimes, to watch with me.
    On Saturday afternoons, he took my little sister and me to buy candy after the football game on teevee. We had to save what we bought until after dinner, which every Saturday night was hamburgers and B&M baked beans. I hated, still hate, baked beans, but I had to eat them even if I cried, until one night I threw up on the little table. Then I didn't have to anymore.

Football is on Sundays, always. Monday night became a big deal, years later, and a break with tradition—so why do I remember football on Saturdays? This isn't a new memory, so I've idly wondered before and forgotten as quickly. Now we have the internet, so I checked the NFL schedule for the 1964 season. Sundays, exclusively. Hmm—then I realized the leagues hadn't merged yet, and my dad would have followed the Boston Patriots in the AFL. I checked the schedule for '64.

Saturdays, like I remembered.

We also got candy, Hershey bars, from an old man who lived on our block. I didn't like chocolate much, but they smelled good and I liked the way the paper unwrapped, so clean and neat. If you ever buy a Hershey bar, I'll unwrap it for you.

Once, a younger man stopped his car and offered us a big clear-plastic lollipop with gumballs inside. We had to (hop in, kids) but we didn't. Clichéd, but it really happened, and it scared my mother badly, badly, badly. I've seen his face since, when other grinning men roll down car windows and look out at a world and the things they claim for their own.

One night, my parents had a fight and the police came and took my mom away in the middle of the night. I watched from my bedroom window as two of them led her up the dark front walk to their waiting squad car. She cooked breakfast the next morning like nothing happened.

Years later, in my 20s, I asked my dad about it when we were drinking and he lied about it. I could see his eyes. He didn't respect people enough to lie to them as a rule, so it was odd. He said I must have dreamed it. I didn't, but I dreamed other things and went places in those dreams.

I don't know if I dreamed more than other toddlers, or if I'm just honest enough to remember my reveries. One sleep, I found myself on the front sidewalk of our L.A house, all alone. My mother's hollyhocks stood in the only patch of hot sun the walnut trees allowed. They nodded at me, pink and white, like they knew something.

Love, Ghost

Santa Claus sat in a chair on our veranda. It took my eyes a moment to adjust to his shade. He had no head. Just loveable Santa in his red fur, enjoying a warm day with no head and no hat. He watched me with his no-eyes and began to laugh. The sound rolled from the neck of his suit, deep and jolly. I can still hear it.

He knew me. He knew every bad thing about me, even if I wasn't old enough to have done anything bad. It made him laugh and laugh. I detoured past the veranda steps and along the side of the house to the back courtyard.

A second monster waited for me there. She had an enormous head, a bald dome, and huge black eyes. Flat rocks joined together to make her skin. A DC comics figure came along later, made of rocks, and it always reminded me of the second monster. Huge, she seemed much more threatening than headless Santa. She stood big, as big as my dad's Pontiac, but I got no sense of proportion. She seemed both near and far.

Her eyes were not quite indifferent, but they held no manipulation. That's the best I can do. They shone, not unkind. All at once I realized what the flat rocks and the hardened skin meant. The monster was a turtle. She spoke in my head. It sounded absolutely natural. The turtle said she belonged to me, and I belonged to her, but neither of us belonged to anyone. Three things were important, she said. I should never forget them.

First—she told me not to worry about Santa, that the headless joker stood for everything real and serious. He would appear again and again throughout my life, but never matter.

Second—my true love lay to the west, so I could never stop walking. If I lost sight of love, I should sit down and wait quietly until sunset. Follow the sinking sun west, and I would never be lost.

Third—she told me your name, Ghost. It's a pretty name, but people always ask you to repeat it when you're

17

introduced, wonder out loud if it's French, then get it wrong anyway.

The turtle made me touch my heart and promise to remember those three things. Then she waved, a kind of benediction, and I woke up. I never saw her again. Not yet, anyway.

The headless Santa has followed me through the years, just as she promised. He mostly finds me on empty streets at night, or when I cry. I've tried not to be too afraid of him. Even when I'm tired, I've never stopped traveling west. I've lost sight of you now, Ghost. Even though you seem gone, I sit quietly and wait for the sun to set.

I still dream about true love and monsters. I remember your name. I whisper it before I fall asleep.

Bob Bickford

Love, Ghost

Dear Ghost,

You told me once, without looking at me, that north is up and south is down. I agreed with you because I always thought so. Almost everyone sees north as up, south as down. Then you said–wait, there's more–east is left and west is right. I could tell by your tone that it was one of those times you wanted to know if I saw the same things you did.

Most people think east is right and west is left, if they think about it at all. I said so, as gently as I could, because I never lied to you. East is right, on every map.

You cast dark eyes my way. "Here, maybe," you said.

Your expression a little sad, because your "here" and everyone else's "here" were different places. You kept one foot in Wonderland.

Last night I walked down a flight of cement steps and landed on dark sand. Across the dark water, to my left, a green light shone. You always loved that light. I don't know who it belongs to or why it's colored so in the eastern sky, but I always turn left and walk toward it until rock tumbles and waves block my way. Then I turn back. The single green light reminds me of you.

It occurred to me last night, paused at the bottom of the steps, that I had to turn left to walk east. The tears came all at once. East is left, after all. You were right. You leave me crumbs of Wonderland, where I'll find them and not forget.

Most people said you were crazy. I knew different. You were Alice, and you knew about the Ocean of Tears and the tea party that's held just beneath the surface of things. You leave bare footprints now, on Askew Beach.

I tell them, imagine the Wonderland hero coming into a nice restaurant where you are halfway through eating something with a French name. She stands in the doorway, scanning faces. She pauses for a moment, silhouetted in the space between night sky and candlelight from the tables, before she spots you and makes her way to your table. Against all the dim elegance, her velvet bow and sash, her thick stockings, the whiteness of her pinafore, all mark her strange. Mark her peculiar.

She approaches smiling, so happy to see you, but the faces in her wake grow alarmed. She trails the faint fragrances of violets and a different century. Conversations hush. Someone sets down a wineglass and knocks it over. A waiter hurries over, clutching a menu in front of him like a shield.

"I've fallen right through the earth," Alice murmurs to him. "How funny it is to come out among people who walk with their heads downwards."

The man nods, uncertain. Even if she's beautiful, Alice is awkward, frightening, and a little bit embarrassing to be seen with. Definitely disordered. You consider asking for the check and making a run for it.

Everything changes when the door opens again. Someone else comes in. You've seen the Red Queen in stories, but nothing has adequately described the malevolence she radiates. Until you're in her presence, there's no way to understand that she's very small, but at the same time so large she has to stoop to get through the entry. Through the open door, the sky over her shoulder has gone bright green, marbled with lightning. The scepter she holds is stained dark with blood.

She gazes around the restaurant, choosing. Somewhere, a shocked fork drops onto a plate.

Across the table from you, Alice rises. Her face is frightened, but resolute. She stands alone against the Queen. Peculiar and crazy are perfectly perfect now. She is afraid of everything, but the bravest person you've ever known. She is the hero you need. She is—glorious.

You realize that you love her, and always have. You are hers.

When we left California and moved to Kansas, I moved to a place where people walked with their heads downwards. I had my Schwinn Sting-Ray and my dogs and a shelf of Hardy Boys books, so I survived.

I remember muddy rivers, and endless corn fields baking green against blue sky. The dirt roads didn't seem to go anywhere. Verandas were wide and cool, with only occasional tornadoes to break the hush.

Mister and Missus Davis had the nicest house in town, a modern ranch shaded by huge elms that looked eternal and didn't imagine the blight coming to kill them. The grass stayed so green and fresh it didn't seem real. The old couple published the Halstead Gazette. Every weekday afternoon at three o'clock on the dot, the paperboys scattered bicycles in their driveway and gathered inside the open garage door to roll and rubber-band and stuff canvas sacks.

I was the youngest of them, by a lot. My dad took me to the newspaper office and got me the job. He told them I acted old for my age.

When the newspapers were ready to roll, everyone got to choose a candy bar from a cardboard box Mister Davis offered around. My mom didn't believe much in candy, and I didn't get it often, so it seemed like impossible riches. Candy, every damn day. I never told her about it. Sometimes, I close my eyes and go into cool shade and the green, green grass, the choice of Three Musketeers or Clark or Butterfinger, and think I've already visited a small corner of heaven.

"Put the wrapper in your pocket," Mister Davis said, every single time. "No littering."

The older boys rolled down the driveway with no-hands, nonchalant. They unwrapped and stuck the candy in the corner of their mouths as they rode off, like the cigarettes they would smoke in a year or two. I chose a different bar every day because I wanted to experience all of them, and I kept mine to look at and eat slowly when I got a few blocks away. I left last, because I didn't want anyone to see me struggle to get my Sting-Ray airborne with the loaded bags slung across the handlebars.

My paper route always ended in time for dinner. I had finished one evening, when in the last few blocks before my house, I saw movement from a purple-gray house where nothing ever moved. The place didn't look as though it ever got the Gazette, or mail, or anything else. A woman came out the front door and crossed the yard. I rode on the sidewalk, but I had been taught pedestrians went first, so I kicked the brake and stopped for her.

The woman looked older, but not old. She had dressed herself for winter, even though it wasn't. She was clad in something else, too. She wore darkness.

She had been wrapped in loneliness, hopelessness, and other empty things. I would find them again later in my life, from time to time, and remember her. She glanced at me from her shadows, then turned left at the end of her front walk. She headed the same way I was going. I followed her because I saw no choices.

I didn't want to get close enough to pass, so I got off my bike and walked it. Her sadness trailed behind her like perfume. When we reached Pine Street, I watched in horror as she angled off the sidewalk and made a beeline for my house.

She began to make a buzzing noise as she headed for a honeysuckle bush that grew on one side, beneath the dining room window. She sounded like a million locusts. She walked directly into the bush, without breaking stride, and disappeared.

Love, Ghost

I dropped my bike on the grass and went to see her. The buzzing got louder as I got close. The woman stood in the very center of the bush, obscured by leaves and blossoms. Only her ankles and shoes were visible at the very bottom. Her pumps were Sunday-shiny. They looked strange in the dirt. Later I would see a movie where a witch got crushed by a house and only her shoes and stockings were visible. It looked exactly like that.

From deep in the honeysuckle, she buzzed and buzzed. I stood paralyzed. In my horror, I fled to a place deep inside me, a place where the grass stayed fresh and green, a place where Frank and Joe Hardy were heroes and rode to rescue pretty girls who wore bright skirts and saddle shoes.

I don't know how long I stayed there, but when I woke up the sky was darker, and the terrible buzzing had gentled into the sound of crickets.

Inside, my mom looked up from the stove.

"You're late," she said. "If you can't be responsible, you can't keep your paper route."

"There's somebody outside in the bushes," I told her. "A lady."

"We won't have this discussion again, Bobby."

She didn't hear me, but my dad did. I might have looked a little pale. He put his bourbon-and-water on the counter and went outside with me. It had gotten nearly dark, but he moved honeysuckle branches around until he felt satisfied nobody hid there. Then he moved my bike from where I had dropped it on the grass to our front steps while I told him the rest.

We walked the couple blocks to the woman's house together. The grass stood high, and the windows were black. He said, gently, that I didn't see what I thought I did, because the house was empty. The lady who owned it had died the year before, so nobody lived there now. We walked back together and didn't say anything else. Along the way, he took my hand even though I was nearly seven years old and too big for it.

I don't know where the woman went. I don't know what she wanted with me. I don't know what terrible anger and sadness drove her, but I never saw her again. I never glanced at the windows when I passed her house.

Somewhere tonight, the woman buzzes and buzzes. She waits for me. I'm not afraid of her though, lovely Alice, because you wait for me, too.

Dear Ghost,

You showed me a report card once. You were eleven when you got it, not little anymore, but before the usual teenaged fever-dreams started. The teacher typed out a nice note, a venomous permanent record. She called you disturbing because you daydreamed a lot, lived in your own world, and didn't seem to care about what went on around you. School apparently mystified and amused you, by turns. No admonishments got through. You needed to straighten up and fly right.

They told you to creative-write an assignment, "Our Family Dog".

You opened: "Of course this dog was not a real one, but the family loved to pretend it was."

That's all you had to say about any family dog, then you segued into a brilliant story about a girl named Alice who lived in a mansion with a sister who was never there. Alice watched the fish in her pond by day, and she heard noises from her kitchen in the middle of the night. Her happily-ever-afters remained undecided, but possible. The End.

The missing family dog outraged the teacher, who said you didn't take things seriously, when in fact the opposite was true. The popular girls obsessed over haircuts and clothes, while you considered the moon. The good girls watched television as you counted waves from shore and attended the slow, icy tracks of the stars.

You were Alice, ever and always. You skipped over their traps and danced on their trip-wires.

The city is different when night fades into the pause before early morning. It stopped raining an hour ago, so colored signs reflect in puddles. A half-mile to the south, skyscrapers rise, lit top to bottom and completely empty. I walk by a fancy bar where I once took a young woman for a drink. I was young, too. She drank a gin-and-tonic. She told me we were over and seemed to find the news exhilarating. The place has a different name, now.

I pass a street where I lived for a little while. The houses are all dark. I wonder what would happen if I turned left and walked two blocks to my old door. Maybe if I tried, I could go inside and my remembered bed would be waiting and I could go to sleep. In the morning, I would make coffee and take back all the heartbreak.

A police car approaches and the tire noise lessens as it pauses to wonder what I'm doing here. I don't make eye contact with the windshield, so it won't sense my sadness and blame me for all the things that should have happened and didn't. The cruiser loses interest and speeds away, but it might be back for me later. A garbage truck rumbles in an alley, yellow parking lights on. I don't know what it's waiting there for. Maybe, like me, its waiting doesn't need a reason.

Only two cigarettes left in the pack and I should save them, but I light one anyway. The taste is confusing because I haven't smoked in decades. The butt sparks when I toss it in the gutter.

A payphone guards the corner of a parking lot, empty at this hour, lit fluorescent, a pale blue Bell stripe on the roof. The phone inside is ringing. I'm suddenly certain the call is for me, so I step over a railing and crunch across broken glass to answer.

The moment I touch the telephone, I can feel your smile from faraway. The receiver gets warm against my ear.

You ask if I recognize your voice. We haven't met, but we knew each other in a different time, another life. You wonder if I remember your laugh, or your favorite shoes, or what you kept in your purse for luck. You wonder if I remember your report card.

I want to play along, but suddenly it isn't play because I do remember you. We met on a streetcar. We both wore

Love, Ghost

uniforms from a war I only ever read about in books, in a city we didn't know. We both peered into the darkness outside the windows and got off at the same wrong stop. I was watching you brush hair back from your cheek, so not really paying attention to the passing avenue. You never needed a reason.

As the last streetcar of the night rumbled away, we stood looking around. There wasn't supposed to be a beach, and the line of docks and black water didn't make sense. When you caught the equally bewildered look on my face, you burst out laughing.

Two dirigibles floated above the docks, barely visible against the night sky, engines at idle. Even if we were strangers, we both loved blimps and you supposed that even wrong stops happened for a reason. We sat on a cement wall and watched the dark ocean. You told me a story about a girl named Alice who lived in a mansion with a sister who was never there. We talked all night, until daylight peeked over the waves and the seagulls wheeled against the new blue and the blimps floated toward the horizon, off to wherever blimps go when the sun comes up.

I tell you now that I remember you eighty-some years ago, but I don't remember your name then. You say it doesn't matter and you have to go, but it's only bye-for-now. Before you hang up, you tell me to stop looking for my heart in the usual places and watch for footprints in the sand. Forever will be along, sooner or later.

You tell me to check the coin return before I leave the booth. After you're gone, I do. I find a single coin, a memento, a promise. I put the tiny streetcar token in my pocket, where it will keep me safe.

I can sleep, now.

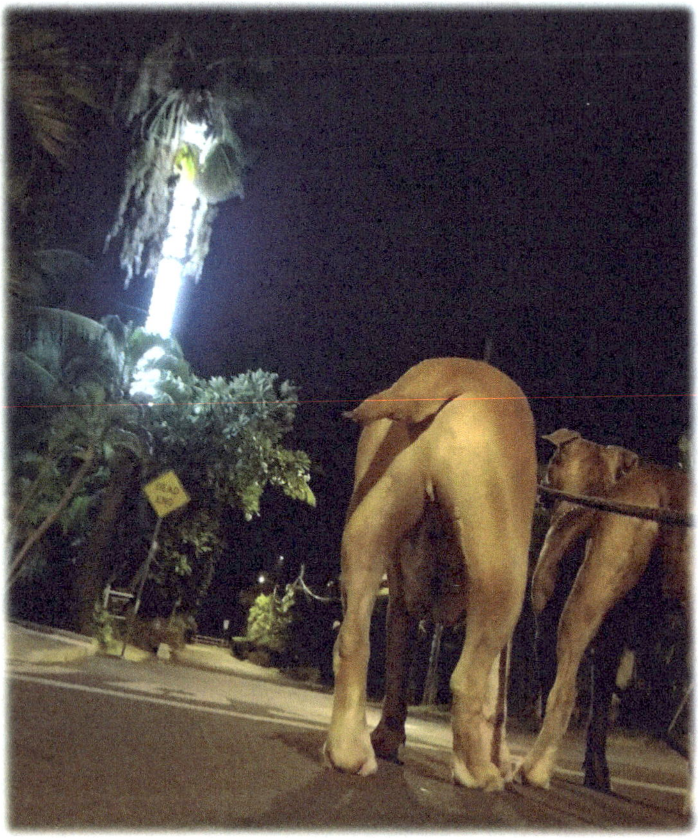

Love, Ghost

Dear Ghost,

    We cut through a park one Fourth of July, on our way to nowhere in particular. I held an open can of orange Fanta, to share. We strolled through kids and dogs, smoky cooking smells and clouds of music. You caught an errant Frisbee one-handed and tossed it back. We passed through a car show on the way out. It wasn't a big deal, just a few dozen old automobiles parked on the grass. The owners squinted behind sunglasses, watching the passersby and hoping to be admired.
    You touched my elbow to stop us in front of a '47 Mercury Eight convertible. You asked the elderly guardian if you might sit in it. Flattered by your good looks, he held the driver door open. You tucked hair behind your ear and lounged for a couple of minutes behind the wheel, very still, looking straight ahead. Your left hand rested at eleven o'clock. Only I knew that you saw things through the windshield glass that were long gone.
    Only I knew why you wept.
    "The burgundy paint looks nice," you wiped your eyes and told him, after you got out. "Mine was green. I bought it brand new. I miss it."
    His smile grew confused. We thanked him good-bye. Fifty yards away, I looked back at him. He still stood, a little stooped, staring after you.
    I knew you before, Ghost–in other years, in other places. We ever dreamed the same dreams, remembered the same things that never happened, knew the maps of places we never lived, missed the same people we never knew. Once upon our time we kissed our so-longs, took off in propeller planes from dirt airfields, and sent telegrams to each other when the missing got too much.

The first time I met you in this life, you didn't say anything to me. You gave me a photograph. I had no idea if I should look at it and give it back, or if it was a strange gift. I tried to find a nice nothing to say. I didn't know you. I didn't understand why you walked up and handed me a Polaroid, so fresh it was nearly sticky. I didn't know why you searched my face with dark eyes before you turned and walked away

You weren't looking for anything from me. Not yet.

I still have that Polaroid on the table beside the bed, where I can see it if I wake up in the middle of the night. I think it got taken standing in front of a dresser, because I can see the edge of a mirror and the lip of a drawer. Seashells and old bits of jewelry are scattered amid scraps of tapestry and tiny paintings. A bird's skull sits with a piece of coral and a few pebbles. Bright colors, a broken charm bracelet, letters, and numbers. Binoculars, a cigar box, a dead Brownie camera, a spray of dried flowers.

For most of the years of my life, I stayed faithful about not keeping mementos or photographs. I never hung pictures on my walls or put knick-knacks on my windowsills. I didn't collect treasures. If I left a place in the middle of the night, I made sure the walls carried no memory of me.

I couldn't miss home if I didn't have one.

Walking into a Greyhound station in the middle of the night made the only real safety I ever knew. One o'clock in the morning washed colors away, so the depots were all the same, in every city. Inside the heavy glass doors, I shifted my backpack and looked around. The terminals were scattered with the kind of people who don't come out in the daytime. They weren't going anywhere on any bus. The station was their home. The tile walls and grimy floors were everything; where they did their dark business, danced to indistinct music, and fell in love.

Love, Ghost

The clerk always appeared utterly exhausted. He gazed at the screen in front of him and sighed. I wondered if he had a kitchen table somewhere where he sat in his nylon vest and tie, looking out a window and waiting for his next shift. Waiting to come back here. He didn't need to look at me because he had seen me before. He had seen everyone before. He already knew my secrets.

I looked at the departure board over his shoulder like it was a menu, a dessert card, a wine list, before I chose Albuquerque or Gulfport or Kansas City. It didn't really matter, because all my roads went west.

I never kept anything, but I kept your Polaroid. You changed everything, with one photograph. You gave me all of the treasures and all of the charms that, when arranged a certain way, come to life. You moved a seashell, scattered a few pieces of colored glass, mixed flower petals with a lock of your hair. You cast a spell over past and future, then and now. I don't travel anymore, because you gave me home.

You're invisible now, but it doesn't matter. In all my dreams, it never stops raining. I stand in the doorway of a closed shop, trying to keep dry, watching the street and waiting for a green Mercury to turn the corner.

I promised not to die first. You promised 1947 would come back.

Bob Bickford

Love, Ghost

Dear Ghost,

I know where you are, right now. You're sitting on a rock, smelling early morning and watching the sun come up to spread every possible color, like spilled paint.
The air feels cool, but the tiny sting on your hair and cheek says it will be hot later. You wait quietly. Maybe you're remembering me, or maybe not. I can read your mind, but I never know what you're thinking.
It's 1981, and the curtain rolls back on a July night. The best part of summer is when it's barely started. A gold Camaro has been pulled around a chained gate, driven deep onto the grass. If the cops spotted the car they'd turn in, but it's weekend so they are busy with other things. I'm sitting on the hood, my heels on the bumper. I hold a bottle of Molson Export on my knee. The beer is getting warm, but I don't really care. There are about twenty more of them in a case on the back seat. I shred the label and scatter confetti into the dark.
Not midnight yet, and Toronto hums and murmurs around me. The bright, loud Saturday night stuff is downtown, well to the south. If the city was a clock, I'd be sitting at eleven, in the dark northwest part, a little off-center. An undeveloped river of grass and brush carries electrical lines through the middle of shopping malls and subdivisions. The giant gantries keep the stores and houses at a distance. Wasted land, and even during the day dog-walkers glance nervously up at the wires and remember this isn't exactly a park.
At night, I have the place to myself.
The car is old and it fills up with exhaust fumes at stoplights, but it has Cragar wheels and a glass pack

muffler. It's a Camaro, no matter what. I wonder if the grass feels good on its tires, after all the miles of hot asphalt. The windows are open, and poor old Stephen Bishop sings from the radio, a song about Jamaica, on and on. Take a ladder, steal the stars from the sky— that sounds pretty good and about right, to me.

There were friends here a little while ago, but they've wandered off. My pretty girlfriend went with them. I have a feeling she'll be wandering off for good, one day soon. I'm mostly okay with all of it. Summertime, I have beer and the perfect dark.

A pale ghost of you lingers, never far away, even if I don't really remember you yet. Even if I don't know your name.

I can't see the electrical towers, but I feel the hum of wires overhead. Far overhead, a plane climbs. The light on its belly seems to change color as it blinks. I lean back to watch it go from east to west. It means something, but I don't know what. I feel like it's leaving me behind.

Half the world away, you rest on a chaise lounge beside a small swimming pool. A big dog lies beside you. You trail fingertips over ears, muzzle, and back. There are underwater lights, but you haven't turned them on. You're fine with the dark, this July night in 1981. You listen to lap and gurgle. You watch the tiny spark of a jetliner move across the sky. It all means something, but you don't know what.

Not yet.

Our mothers and fathers look out at us from old photographs. They play records, smoke cigarettes, and laugh. On bright warm days, they don't believe their skies and trees and grass will turn black-and-white, or that hot sun, cold water, music, can fade. They have Saturday night dances and falling in love planned. They never imagine being anyone's ancestors.

Love, Ghost

We don't believe it either, but somehow, we've gotten old, anyway. I don't drink beer these days. The gold Camaro is long asleep in the corner of some junkyard. The perfect summer afternoons still move though, and the jetliners still blink in night skies, east to west. I'm still looking for you, Ghost.

Steal your money and break your heart. If I could explain that, I'd have the answer to everything.

Bob Bickford

Love, Ghost

Dear Ghost,

You asked me once about my life, the parts when you hadn't been around. We sat on a flight of steps above the beach. Four o'clock in the morning, and the cement felt cool beneath my legs. The ocean ran a little rough, shore lights glinting on the waves as they rolled in.
"What was it like, without me?" you asked. "Start at the beginning and tell me everything."
"There's not much to tell," I said. "Not really."
"What did you do before me?"
I didn't have the slightest idea what you were asking, and I didn't want to think about it. Most of the things you said to me didn't make perfect sense until much later. You had your Alice ways.
"I don't want to hear the middle," you clarified. "The middle never matters. The real story is always the beginning—and the end."
I took your hand and stepped onto the beach without answering, because we planned a long walk before sunrise. You let go of me and danced on the sand, your question apparently forgotten. I wish I could have that moment back.
I'd tell you my life without you is a small city that sits on a warm sea. I'd say my life now is coastal. I'd say the boats leaving the harbor are small. I'd mention the dogs prowling the streets and lounging in shaded doorways because you like dogs. I'd tell you about curtains of bougainvillea hanging from railings and not much else happening.
The beaches are black sand, lined with seaberries and spider lilies. Palm trees rattle and murmur in hot breezes. There are no hotels on the strand because tourists never come here. The natives mostly just get by. There are no sidewalks, and the streets are full of old pickup trucks. In

the evenings, radios get set on balconies so the streets are also full of music. It all smells of salt and rot.

There have been earthquakes. You can see the damage, here and there.

Buildings got knocked down or washed away, and none of them will ever get repaired. Some parts of town, people carry water every day in buckets. The pipes are damaged too badly to fix, so they'll probably haul water to drink and cook and wash as long as they live. It's better than moving. The city is always a little bit less because it can't be rebuilt the way it used to be. There isn't enough wood, and we're low on cement.

Most of all, there isn't time.

I think about the people I've lost. I think about the early morning phone calls, the doctors who speak without letting go the handles of waiting room doors, the kisses given to someone else, the slammed receivers and angry goodbyes. They all left without warning, my loves, even if there were omens and telegrams I should have opened.

Every single time, I knew things might get good again but they'd never be like they were.

When a roof blows off and walls tumble, I let the kudzu grow, drag canvas chairs and umbrellas into the rubble, pour a beer and call it a patio. The waves knock down the pier and change the beach, so I sunbathe on new sand, admire my sunburn, and say change is as good as a vacation.

That's my life, Ghost. It's beautiful and broken. Dogs, busted pipes, and rusty pickup trucks. A hell of a lot of earthquakes.

One day I'll be staring at nothing, thinking about you, when the whole thing slides into the sea. It will go under without much fuss. When the waves subside, the sea will still be turquoise. The sun will still be hot enough to bleach the blue sky. An occasional bubble will break the surface. Pelicans will head off toward distant roosts.

Love, Ghost

It will all still be beautiful. More than ever, maybe. We'll be mermaids then, you and I.

Bob Bickford

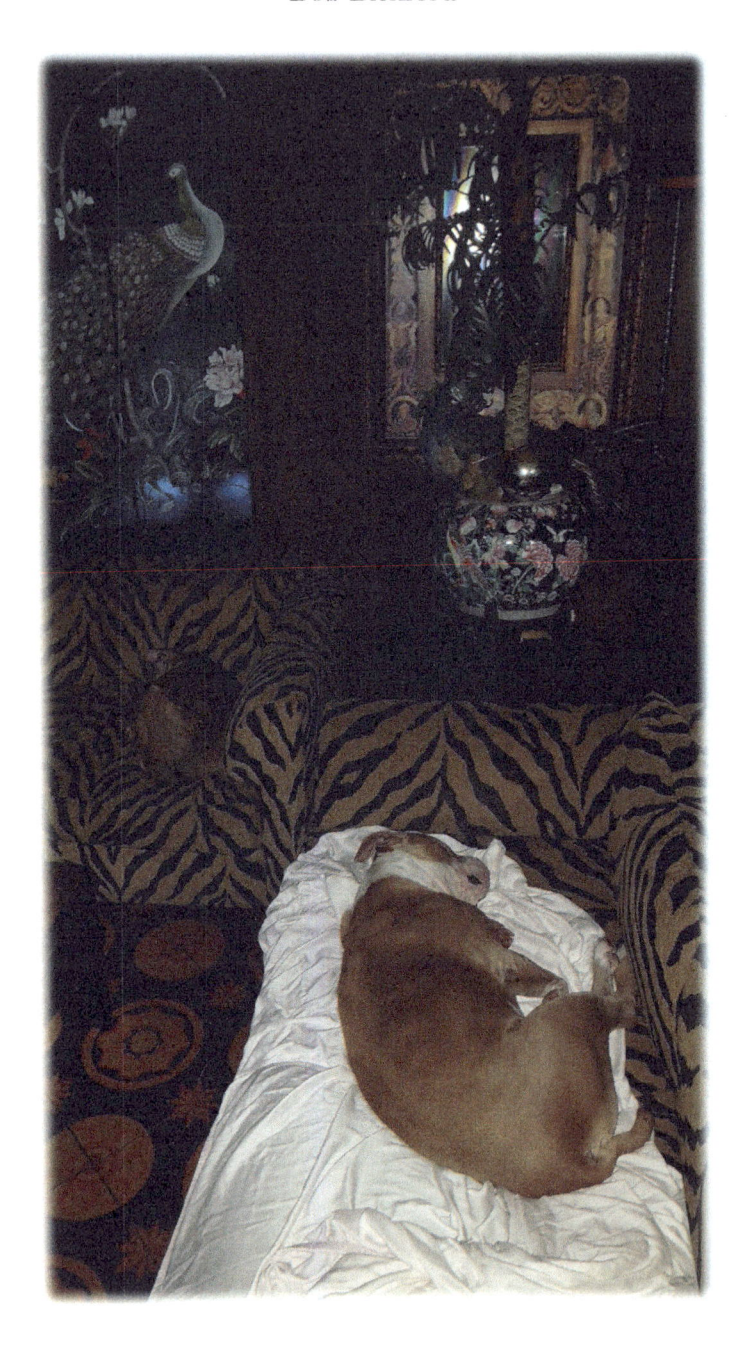

Love, Ghost

Dear Ghost,

I'm standing on a sidewalk, about two hours north of Los Angeles. Behind me, a 7-Eleven, the parking lot empty. Things are different here, early in 1983, where Route 66 runs into the Pacific Ocean and disappears.

The end of the road came about eleven the night before. After a couple days of flat interstate across New Mexico and Arizona, the bus struggled up the steep California grades, shuffling gears like a card trick that kept coming up wrong. The big Greyhound developed an exhausted rattle, one that got louder after Ventura. The driver finally pulled it onto the shoulder, like a horse that needed to rest.

Too black outside the windows to see the ocean, but I could feel it.

Passengers stirred in the dark, craning to look forward. Nobody spoke up because everyone understood that asking questions might make the situation real. A replacement bus out of the L.A terminal would take hours, if it ever came at all. The kind of people who took buses didn't have better options, so Greyhound didn't care how long they had to wait.

A Motel 6 sign glowed above us, a little way south. I wanted a hot shower and I needed a mattress to sleep on, so I shrugged on my backpack. The driver wasn't supposed to let me out on the freeway, but he decided he didn't care, either. The door hissed open. I waded through desert scrub and hopped a chain link fence to get to the road that climbed to the motel.

Now it's morning. I return the room key a little before six. After sprawling in a bus seat for three days, I don't need more sleep. I do need cigarettes. A little way down the frontage road, I spot the 7-Eleven and start walking.

The coming sun is enough to gray the warm air, but not enough to turn out the streetlights. The dark expanse downhill to my left is the Pacific, but I'll have to wait a little while longer to see it.

I ask the guy behind the counter for a pack of Kool Lights, and he asks me for seventy cents. It seems like a fair trade, familiar and comforting in this strange place. I give him a single and he pauses a long moment before dipping fingers into the coin tray, like he's lost track. He's tired, and pretty ordinary-looking for this adventure, like he ought to be teaching high school kids geography, not manning a 7-Eleven just before six o'clock in the morning. I probably look like one of his students.

We aren't those things, though. Maybe we were once, but not now.

A radio plays on the counter behind him. Rita Coolidge sings a Boz Scaggs standard softly, so she won't disturb the early morning hush. We're all alone, she tells me. Close the window. I like the song, and I like it even more coming from a California radio station. I glance around at the stainless hot dog grill, the stacks of newspapers, the bright rows of candy bars, like I might want something else. I just want to stay until the end of the song. The geography teacher eyes me funny, so I settle for playing it in my head and head back out the glass doors.

Close your eyes and dream. We're all alone, Rita sings. Always alone, and never alone.

I slit cellophane, scratch lighter, get a cigarette started. The air feels soft, the sun has crept up. I get my first look at the Pacific Ocean, spread out on the other side of the 101 freeway. I haven't seen it since I was little. The dark water is calm, tinted pink at the edges.

You talk to me, Ghost. If a 7-Eleven can overlook such perfect beauty, you say, then anything is possible, here at the end of my road.

Love, Ghost

The bald-tire Nova parked beside the building might have been blue once, before sun and the salt air got to the paint. No doubt it belongs to the guy behind the counter. He's been up all night, cleaning the Slushie machine and making coffee. He probably has a wife as tired as he is, and a couple of kids who go to school in cheap sneakers. It doesn't matter how hard he works

I need a guy to sell me cigarettes at six in the morning a lot more than I need a millionaire who trades stocks or flips properties. If I ran the world, the geography teacher would be driving a Ferrari. It doesn't cross my mind he has a lot more than I do. I'm down to sixteen bucks, so tonight I'll either find a hostel or sleep on the beach.

The truth is, it's all pretty damn romantic. The Pacific is catching new light, and you're whispering in my ear. I just don't know what to do, now I'm here.

I also don't know I'm going to get a job later today, washing cars. I'll spend the next dozen or so years here beside the sea, waiting for a sign. Waiting for you. I don't know your name, what you look like, or the sound of your voice, but my heart got spoken for a long time ago.

We spin through the middle of a wild universe, a party for stars and planets and forces too big to understand. We're eternal, even if we don't understand what eternal is. I'm small. My job was the Pacific Ocean. I did it, and I'm here.

I finish my cigarette and start walking. You're around the very next corner, Ghost.

Always alone, and never alone.

Bob Bickford

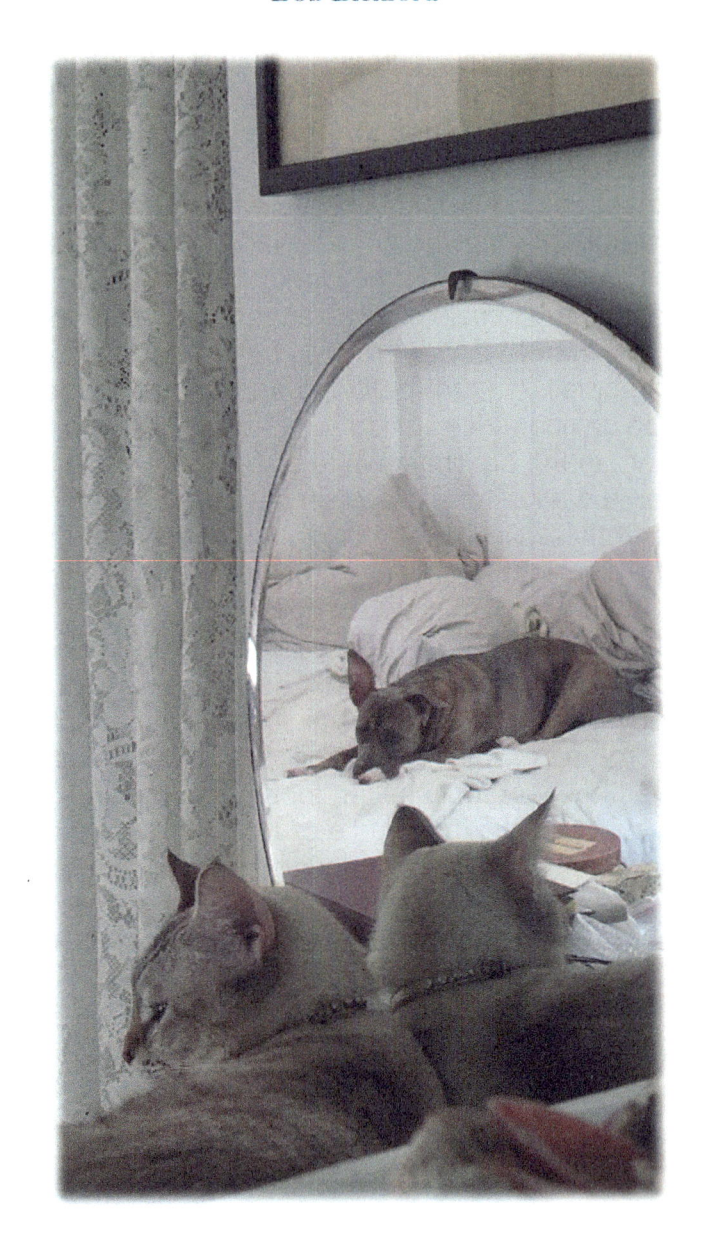

Love, Ghost

Dear Ghost,

You broke my heart, more than once.
I think you wanted me to be ready, and you imagined it would help me later. A heart can't be broken twice, you thought. I didn't need the help. I could have told you a heart can get broken a thousand times.
Two months into Grade 4, I got pulled out of class and sent to the principal's office. It wasn't the first time, but it was the first time my mom waited there. She wore perfume and a dress.
"I believe," the principal told me, "that your behavior problems have their roots in your not being sufficiently challenged."
He smoothed his hair, walked to his office window, stood looking out. My mom was pretty, so he was showing off. He knew his solution pleased her.
"When you go back to class, empty your desk," he said. "Tomorrow, you'll join the Grade 5 classroom. I believe a more difficult curriculum will keep you busy and out of trouble."
I had too many challenges, already. I saw ghosts and sensed the world was more transparent than anyone knew. It would be decades before I found out I wasn't alone because you saw the same things, too. I didn't need more challenges, but I had no nine-year-old way to tell them that, and they wouldn't have listened.
The Grade 5 teacher was a man named Mister Breeze. He met me at the classroom door and told me that he didn't think my new placement was a very good thing for anyone, especially me, but we would make the best of things and I was welcome. I'm not sure if he ever spoke to me again.
He wore thick eyeglasses and sweaters with buttons. In my memory, he is an old man, but he was barely out of

teacher's college. Sometimes, we remember people as they really were. He seemed like a careful man who took everything seriously. Careful included teaching and flying his little airplane on weekends. He devoted himself to both.

My new classmates were mystified by me. The gulf between nine and ten years old is unimaginable. After a while, they realized I wasn't going to do anything interesting, so they ignored me. After school, I went back to Cub Scouts and pee-wee hockey with my Grade 4 friends. They decided I was some kind of a freak and ignored me, too.

I didn't belong anywhere anymore, so I sat alone at recess, thinking about things. Sometimes I brought a book with me. I found out I didn't mind not belonging.

I only belonged to you. Maybe I knew that, even then.

Mister Breeze went to the airport on Saturdays with his best friend, who also owned a plane. They took off in their little Cessnas and flew around. Afterward, they talked about revolutions-per-minute and wingspans, and did whatever airplane people do on a Saturday afternoon when the flying is done.

During the week, he taught us a little about flight. We learned the principles of thrust and lift. The simplicity, the beauty of it, delighted him. He promised us we would build airplanes with what we had in our desks: notebook paper skins, toothpick spars, white glue. He impressed on us that the magic lay in careful mathematics and precise measurements. Too much glue, a spar the wrong angle, and the spell would break. If we did everything right, he promised our planes would actually fly. They would be real.

The airplanes made slow, picky work. I think we probably did flight lessons when we were supposed to be doing geography or mathematics, but over the course of that fall semester I managed to finish both wings and was ready to start the fuselage.

Love, Ghost

One Monday, Mr. Breeze came to class after his usual weekend flying. After a skate around the sky, he had followed his friend's little Cessna back to the airport. A jetliner a mile ahead of them landed, leaving invisible eddies of air. The leading plane got caught in wake turbulence, and his best friend fluttered to the ground and died. Mr. Breeze, in the trailing airplane, watched his friend hit the earth.

I considered my meticulously glued toothpicks and wondered if the young pilot had looked at his aircraft the same way. I wondered if he firmly believed in being careful, and in the principles of aerodynamic flight. I wondered he realized, as the ground spun up to meet him, that sometimes life is sad and it doesn't matter how careful you are.

Maybe Mr. Breeze wasn't supposed to tell us about his friend. Maybe we were too young. Maybe he had to tell someone and had nobody else. Maybe I was the only one who listened, and the only one who remembers them today.

We didn't finish our airplanes. They stayed in our desks and just weren't mentioned again. There were no more flight lessons. I think most of the kids were tired of tiny measurements before they glued a toothpick, anyway. I took the wings home with me at the end of the year. I planned to finish the airplane by myself. Of course, I never did. Still, I kept the paper wings for a few years. I still think about them sometimes and wonder where they are now.

The flying lesson remains one of the few gifts school ever gave me. If we're ever in terrible trouble, Ghost, as long as we have enough toothpicks and glue, I'll build an airplane and fly us out. When it's most dangerous, I'll always make you laugh. I promise.

It also taught me that sometimes even when we're careful, the earth spins up to meet us. I think it's important to know that not all sad things happen because someone is wrong. Sometimes hearts just have to break.

    I looked for you my whole life. I only have paper wings, and nothing else.

Bob Bickford

Love, Ghost

Dear Ghost,

One of these days, I'll wake up and swing my feet out of the bed. The window will show gray sky, and I'll move down the hall for my cautious shower.
Propped beneath warm water, I'll read the soap label. It promises the fragrances of hibiscus, sea kelp, and marine minerals. None of those things smell like soap, but this smells nice so there's no point in finding fault with little things. I rarely comb my hair or wear clothes with buttons these days, but I like to smell clean.
Carbolic soap is the cleanest smell I know, but it's made from coal—terrible dead stuff. Washing with perfumed seaweed seems like a better choice. I don't know if anyone even sells carbolic soap these days.
Gray T-shirt, baggy old shorts, and my baseball cap. Like me, they've seen better days.
A lot of Augusts have gone by since I sat behind first base at Fenway and watched an unknown named Roger Moret pitch against Chicago. In the seventh inning, an infield bouncer popped out of Doug Griffin's glove, so a no-hitter turned into a one-hitter and the perfect afternoon game got ruined. My dad slapped his forehead, said it should have been called an error, and we almost saw history. I'll never forget the ugly noise from the crowd, the gray smoky sound of violence, equally angry at the ump and the second baseman.
I've stayed wary since, of people who wear the same colors.
Roger Moret got found catatonic in the showers just before he was supposed to start a 1978 game against Detroit. He tried a couple games after he got out of the

psych hospital, but he was done. He disappeared back to Puerto Rico and died not-quite-old. I don't know if he stayed crazy.

We all manage crazy, time to time, but we don't all manage glory. You were magnificent, Roger. The infield single was an error. In heaven, they know that.

Ring of keys, coins, and my wallet get left on the bedside table. They make a little treasure map, a letter for anyone who knows how to read it. I go to the dresser drawer and hunt up the wristwatch I haven't worn in years. Too nice for every day, added to the pile it makes things just right.

I consider for a moment, then I fish a single dime from the change and pocket it. I'll need it, for the bus.

I should feel sad, but I don't. I always hated to be the one left behind, but excited to be the one leaving. That's a kind of selfishness, I know, and unfair. Maybe I needed more time, if I was going to learn to be good.

Outside, 1963 Los Angeles goes about its business. The end is the beginning, and I'm back where I started from. I glance back at my front door, closed behind me. Closed forever, present day gone for good, but that's all right. Down the steps and I barely make the sidewalk before a green-and-white bus turns the next corner, all puffs of black smoke and art deco lines.

The driver wears a flight cap and bow tie. I put my dime in his little glass-sided box and ask him where we're going.

"You see the sign said 'Sunset and Vine' when you got on, pal?"

"I guess I didn't read the sign," I say. "I'm new here."

"Do me a favor and clear the aisle, would you?"

A young woman sits across from me—hat, stiletto heels, and nylon stockings. A shaved poodle leans against her legs. The dog watches me. The woman makes it a point not to. The open window behind her brings me a hint of the Wind Song she's wearing. I don't really know perfume, but my mother wore it, when I was little.

I pull the cord to ring the bell when I spot the white towers of the Trianon Apartments. Douglas Fairbanks had the Hollywood castle built for Mary Pickford, a place for them to live happily ever after. He didn't build it himself, of course. Workers who took the streetcar from Newport and Buena Park built it. The newlyweds just drove up in a Hispano-Suiza and moved in when it opened. I never trusted the joy in marble floors and vases of flowers if I didn't put the toilets and sinks in myself.

I always wondered why he commissioned her an apartment building instead of a mansion. They must have needed people around, to build a home where a lot of strangers could live with them. Maybe there's nothing wrong with that.

An alley runs behind the building. I turn in. The midday sun off white stucco makes me squint. A green door is set into the opposite wall, a little way down. Most of the paint has peeled off, and the bare wood feels warm beneath my palm. Vines tumble over the top of the wall, dotted with delicate star-shaped flowers.

The door is unlocked. You're curled up behind it, on a wicker loveseat, a book in your lap.

I knew about the garden inside. I expected the cool air, the plumeria blossoms and the running water. I remembered the fish, and the shower trees dropping yellow petals into all the green. I didn't know your eyes would be exactly the same, though. I've never known what to expect, with you.

"Been a long time," I say.

"Has it?" You watch my face and consider that. "I've been reading."

Maybe it hasn't been long for you, all the years I sat in front of news programs and made dinner and did the dishes and got old. Maybe forever time is different. You have a cup of coffee at your elbow. Tiny white curdles float on the surface. I know you've let it get cold, so in a little while you'll take the cup inside and reheat it. Then you'll let it get cold again. You always did.

I sit on the edge of the fountain. We stay quiet for a little while. Seeing you is enough and doesn't need conversation.

"Maybe we'll go to the beach," you finally say. "Later—we have time, now. I'll buy you an ice cream. Maybe you'll take off your shoes and socks and leave them behind on the sand, and we'll wade into the surf. Maybe I'll catch your elbow—stop here—and tell you I've been waiting to kiss you."

A small plane buzzes, high in the overhead blue. I hear Casey Kasem, very faintly, from an unseen radio. I remember the song, but not the words.

"This is a good day," I say.

You sip your cold coffee and nod. I know you're happy, too.

Bob Bickford

Love, Ghost

Dear Ghost,

Kansas summer, and people still scan twilight skies for tornado clouds, even though the threat of them fades when kitchen calendars flip to July. Walter Cronkite recites the Vietnam death toll every evening in black-and-white, while hamburgers fry in the kitchen. Tuesday night, so "Rat Patrol" will be on later.

When it gets dark, my granddad will burn the trash in a steel barrel back by the alley. I watch from the upstairs bedroom window. There's a glow-in-the-dark hot rod model on the shelf, keeping me safe. Every now and then, he pokes the fire with a stick and sparks shoot up, echoes of the fireflies bobbing through the back yard.

It's dark, but there are lights everywhere if you know where to look.

Tomorrow, there will be swimming. We'll throw rolled towels into our bike baskets and ride down Main Street to the grain elevators. Bump off the curb onto dirt road, bank left and follow the railroad tracks to the public pool.

A nickel admission at the window, then two pennies for long strings of purple licorice at the snack bar. I hate black licorice with my whole heart, so grape feels like a magic spell, a way to turn something bad into something wonderful. I can still taste it. Bare feet, and the cement feels hot under the wet. The teenaged girls tan with iodine mixed into Johnsons' Baby Oil. I know their rituals—oil on hot skin, the hitching and snapping of bikinis—are essential and central, even if I'm too young to understand what they mean.

I've wasted time and done a lot of things entirely wrong, Ghost—but I've always known what matters and I never once asked why.

The water is cold and blue, the afternoon feels hot on shoulders. My towel is soaking wet but warm from the sun so I don't mind. Line up for the diving board, slip on the ladder. It all smells of chlorine and coconut butter. It's my favorite place.

One afternoon, some Mexican kids went swimming. I was there that day, but I didn't notice them in the pool. The next day, a sign got pinned up beside the pay-window that said some people couldn't come in. Town ordinance.

I told my mom about the sign and she said no goddamned way. No fucking way. Those sons of bitches—this will not stand. This is 1967, not 1867—and this will not stand. She gathered her spells, her guitar, her flower-power, and her Volkswagen Beetle, then she stood against hatred and she stood against the town. I don't know much about her crusade because that's the way she wanted it, but I know she lost.

We moved away. There are lots of different ways to tar-and-feather a person and drive them outside the walls, into the dark. That story is mostly lost now, the smells and sounds and colors that make a story real too faded to bring back to life, but I know as much as I need to.

I know what matters. I remember, and I never ask why.

Sometimes, knights dress themselves in light. Some knights are glow-in-the-dark. My mom carried a lance, all wound with flowers. She was small, pretty, and maybe more than a little crazy. I'm glad I knew her. I miss her. I hope I see her again.

Maybe we'll invite her for lunch one day, Ghost. You'd like each other, I think.

Hatred is a different kind of knight. He rides a big horse through the streets. He wears hair spray and a necktie beneath his cardboard suit of armor, and he knows hearts. He likes the small towns best, the ones where people fly flags from their front verandas and drive pickup trucks. Ray Bradbury knew that. He warned us that the Martians make a point of looking just like us. We didn't listen.

Love, Ghost

Hatred sits relaxed in his saddle. He carries a cross in the crook of one elbow. The people who belong to him come out of their houses and stand on the curbs to cheer as he rides by. They shake their fists, proclaim victory, shout themselves hoarse with praise, and swoon at his beauty. He turns his head, left and right, to look at them and remember their names.
Beneath his cardboard helmet, he has no face. The crowd doesn't notice or doesn't care. Then Hatred is past, headed for the highway, leaving behind the smell of smoke and a cloud of flies. The righteous ones ruffle the pages of the books they don't read and wipe the sweat from their necks. Then they go back inside their houses, to snap down the shades and bask in warm gloom.
The sun comes out again. The lovely summer comes back. The dogs stop barking and circle back into cool spots to nap. Air conditioners rattle and hum and drip water from bedroom windows. The sprinklers start up, their back-and-forth rainbows arcing every color against the hot, blue sky. The blight hasn't come along yet to kill all the elm trees, so they still bless these dirt streets with shade.
In my memories and in my dreams, you're in Kansas with me. I never left you behind in California, Ghost. I carry you with me, every day, forever. All by yourself, you watch the spot Hatred rode into. Even when you're with me, sometimes you're alone. Dark eyes, light hair, you straddle your bike, one foot up on a pedal.
You ride a purple Sting-Ray with tassels streaming from the handle bars. The purple paint has sparkles, and there are more tiny sparkles mixed into the white plastic seat cover. For the rest of my life, when I see sparkles, I'll think about you. Your dad put a racing slick tire on the back wheel, like the boys use. You're skinny and you're a dancer, but you're serious about your bike and you ride faster than all the boys.

Except me, sometimes. On the days I wash my bike with the hose and pump my tires at the gas station and drip my dad's can of 3-in-One oil on my chain, you let me win. You were always kind.

Now you watch the distant thunderhead of flies. The things nobody else sees will haunt you every day of your life. You gaze at the sun-shimmer over the highway leading out of town, while clouds move across your eyes. You break my heart, now and always.

"Let's go downtown, Lefty," I tell you. "Get some ice cream. I have a quarter."

You watch the road a moment longer. Then your eyes move over, in the sweet, easy way you have, to read my face. That glance will just about stop my heart when we're older. Your smile starts slow, then bursts.

"I thought you were saving that quarter for my birthday," you say.

You're teasing me, but you're also serious and I don't know how you knew I was saving it—but I don't know how you know all sorts of things. I give it some thought.

"Every day is your birthday," I tell you. "So, let's get ice cream."

It doesn't need to make sense to be my truth, Ghost. I want to throw good things at you, like confetti. I want to make you forget the smell of smoke.

You're painted with light. All my days are your birthday.

Bob Bickford

Love, Ghost

Dear Ghost,

You lost someone.
He had been there every day of your life since you were little. Young and good-looking, he drove fast cars and flew airplanes. The sun painted his skin gold and he swam in the ocean. He laughed and put the needle down on records, mixed martinis at sunset, and he always knew what to do. You sat in the seat behind him in his small airplane, and it felt scary-safe. He loved you and his hands adjusted flaps and throttle and you would never fall from the sky, because he was the pilot.
You grew up and somehow, he got old. He walked slowly and talked slowly and spent more time looking at the sky. He was still a pilot though, even if his plane wasn't around. When he talked to you, you still knew you wouldn't fall.
Then you got a twilight phone call, and they told you he left. We forget so many good moments, we can't remember the smell of the flowers our beloveds wore, but we never forget those phone calls.
You told me: "Scared and sad. It's different walking out the door. East. He's gone."
In his last days, you saw him on the street sometimes when everyone else was asleep, hands behind his back, gazing up at the dark. You thought he couldn't sleep and couldn't fly anymore, so he was remembering the clouds. Seeing him that way, so old, hurt your heart.
You told me that every morning he touched Amelia Earhart and sent a secret salute to Charles Lindbergh.
I figure he was checking the weather, the prevailing winds, or whatever things flyers check. Good pilots are careful. They don't make an evening flight without

memorizing conditions. They love the sky, and the sky loves them.
He was getting ready to fly again.
A part of your life leaves with him. A part of your story ends. That's sacred, not sad, because he folds your pages carefully, stows you in his leather map-case, and tucks you behind the pilot seat. Safe.
He has a Labrador dog as copilot, and he leans forward to looks out at you—a look to last a while—and sees you little again, standing and waving. Then the propeller spools up and the plane trundles out to find the taxiway. They always look awkward on the ground, like fat little dogs following their noses, don't they? Blinking red light catches a thermal at the end of the runway and bounce-bobs a little bumblebee thing before the wings claw at the sky.
The plane catches air and suddenly isn't awkward anymore. It climbs out over the water. You follow the flashing light with your eyes (wait don't go) until it's lost in the warm dark.
You'll still hear the engine sometimes when you least expect it. Summer isn't summer without Casey Kasem on the radio and the sound of a Cessna following the beach. The sound will fill the sky, sweet and faint, so you'll look up.
Someday, you'll hear a plane and spot white wings banking out over the water. Your story is coming back for an ending, back for safe landing on the Hopeloa tarmac. You'll smile because it's all scary but the pilot won't ever let you fall.
Part of you is gone, for now. That's okay. It's supposed to be that way. That's what love is.

Bob Bickford

Love, Ghost

Dear Ghost,

Ask me if we'll live forever, and I'll point to July.

1979: Toronto is hot, but the alleys surprise you with leafy green in the dirtiest concrete corners. Every doorway has "Sultans of Swing" playing from a radio, and they sell fruit from beneath awnings on the sidewalk. The people who head to work on the subway, loosened ties and pink flushes beneath makeup, seem bound for a beach holiday. They'll find a park to eat lunch in, today. It's hard to find parking at the beer store. The breeze smells of hot dogs with mustard, and the ocean a thousand miles away.

I have the weekend, new Levis, the keys to a small Italian car, and an entire Burger King paycheck in my pocket. The possibilities are sweet, endless, aching.

Dusk falls. Since I'm giddy with July, I call a young woman, a crush completely out of my league. She's the kind of pretty that makes you glad just to be in the same room, on the same planet, using the same calendar. We have mutual friends, the same summer crowd. I'm hopelessly smitten, but I would never, ever tell her so.

The phone rings twice, and she answers. I was expecting her mother to tell me she was out. I don't have any babble prepared.

(Have you heard from so-and-so? I ask. Things are probably happening somewhere tonight. If we both happened to go to the same place, with the same group, could you use a ride?)

She's not busy, and she would like a ride to whatever fun things our group is doing.

(That sounds great. See you in an hour.)

She said 'yes'. Not a date, not exactly, but I'm happy to settle for giving a ride and spending an evening in her orbit. Only trouble is, I haven't heard from anyone else in the group today and can't find them now. I don't have a clue what fun things are probably happening somewhere. I make sure I have change, because I'll need to find a payphone after I pick her up and hope like hell someone answers. This could be embarrassing. This might be a disaster, on a scale I can't imagine.

I pause on the step. I should call her back and tell her everyone canceled, that there's nowhere to go. See you tomorrow, maybe? I should save myself.

The little car sits on the street though, freshly washed and fat-tired, looking like it came from a twisty road in Monaco. I have a Burger King paycheck, freshly cashed. The planters next door are full of flowers, and the street feels like summer might burst it.

I never say no to July, not then and not now. Let's go.

She opens the door looking like a warm wind poster, shorts and light tan—gee, your hair smells terrific. I've never seen anything like her, not in movies, not in dreams. She's different, somehow. Her brand of beautiful is concentrated tonight, more than I can make sense of. I realize it's how she's looking at me. She asks

(What should we do?)

Her eyes are blue, they hold mine, and the message is clear. This is for me. She uncapped lipstick and looked at herself in the mirror, just for me. I'm stunned. She asks, again

(What should we do?)

Maybe I hadn't thought this was a date, never in a million years—but she did. Our summer crowd isn't even mentioned, let alone invited.

I open the car door for her. It's a ceremony that binds us, at least for a little while. The foreign engine snarls and spits and snaps away from stoplights. It sounds happy, in Italian. There are no plans, but it doesn't matter. A four-hour walk downtown. The night is full of Carly Simon and David Bowie and the Electric Light Orchestra. The colored

Love, Ghost

lights are haloed, the air smells like good food, and it's all nearly too much.
I look at the rest of my life and think:
This is going to be pretty good.

July faded into November. The rain started, the faces changed, the promises got broken, and we went our separate ways. The summer crowd scattered. We got older, year after year. We detoured into jobs and mortgages, health scares, bad habits and worse decisions, property. We chased empty horizons, the things we expected to want. We got lost. We have a pile of paper full of fine print and numbers these days, but the little Italian car went to the crusher, a long time ago.

We don't drink beer and we don't bother with lipstick. Not anymore. We thought we could head back to July when we got everything else done. We thought 1979 would wait for us to be ready. It didn't.

I didn't even know your name back then, Ghost. You were a whole ocean away, so I wasn't sure if you were real. I didn't know then that real doesn't matter.

I want to shake off the strange places, the scrape of footsteps on cement, the nights when the streetlights look cold, the dead trees. I want to lose the suspicion I don't believe in anything. I want warm water lit by sun, the orange smell of cut mango, honeyed skin, and honeyed words caught in the back of my throat. I want eyes so dark they're nearly black. I want summer-sweet Alice-nonsense nobody understands, set to music.

Sometimes, the way back to the beginning is to start at the end.

A door stands ajar. You're inside, curled up and reading a letter I wrote you a long time ago. The dog stretches out, across your feet. She opens one eye to look at me, then goes back to sleep. There are books, a waterfall of plants, sunlight through colored glass, and the sound of running water.

I've passed this doorway a thousand times, but I realize I've never seen this room before. I smile a little because everything is 1979.
I look for just a moment, trying to memorize you. Then I keep going, outside to feed the fish. I don't need to disturb you, and we never talk out loud, anyway. It was you, the whole time, Ghost. You were always July.
I look at the rest of my life and think:
This is going to be pretty good.

Bob Bickford

Dear Ghost,

I'm thinking about where we could live someday, if nothing was any object—if we had no problem with time, if we didn't have to worry about getting old and nobody died first, and neither of us had to figure out what to do if we got left behind. We'll find an empty place, somewhere everyone else has forgotten.

When I turned ten, we lived for a couple years in a small town outside of Toronto. Our rented house was much more modern and contemporary than we were used to.

My parents saw some strange things in that house, once in an upstairs hallway and another time just outside the front door. They wondered to each other, in low murmurs, if such a new house could be haunted. I could have told them, but they never asked me.

A woman named Deanne lived by herself in the bungalow across the street. Painted pale blue, her house had been set into a hillside in no particular order. The rooms seemed to have been perched wherever the slope allowed. She drove a brand new 1970 Plymouth Duster, the "Twister" model, bright orange with a 360 engine and cartoon tornados on the front fenders. She had big hair and hips that stretched her pants in a way that I vaguely understood was dangerous.

My mom sometimes looked across the street and wondered how a hairdresser owned her own home and drove a car like that. She had to be doing more than styling hair. My mom probably meant to be mean, but she didn't say it in a mean way. She said it like a pretty young woman with a lot of kids looking wistfully at an off-ramp she'd missed, a secret she'd been locked out of, a closed door.

On Saturday mornings, various men parked across the street and got out of Chargers and Mustangs. They carried cases of beer up the long flight of front steps. I had the whole weekend to admire their Hot Wheels cars come to life and hope I'd be like those men, someday.

Nobody warned me to be careful what I wished for.

Deanne didn't have a back yard. She just had a grassy hill. She also didn't have fences. If I dropped my bike in our driveway and crossed the street, I could loop around the rear bumper of her orange Duster and go around the furthest of her additions, into the tall grass. She saw me once from her front window, and she gave me a little wave to say it was okay.

I had no reason to climb the hill, except kids don't tend to leave grassy hills unclimbed.

Near the top, a scraggle of woods grew like a rampart. No path led through the trees, or at least I never found one. Do the breaststroke and try not to get an eye poked with a branch. When the forest thinned and I came back into sunshine, the other side of the hill stretched for—miles.

There were no houses or roads, no farm fields, no telephone wires—just green in every direction. Good grasses moved like water when the wind blew across them. Clumps of trees stood here and there, as if they had spotted me and waited. I felt immediately sure that I was the first person who had seen the place.

A distant sparkle of water blinked the sun at me, like a secret message. I went there first and found a brook, amber water running clear over pebbles. The water sang and ran slow, pausing in small pools and playing in tiny waterfalls.

The trees seemed like places to live. If I packed a lunch, I could walk across the green all the way to the Pacific Ocean, without seeing a building or a sidewalk. It wasn't a place to bring my friends. I only went up the hill when I felt sure nobody saw me.

Love, Ghost

All the times I climbed the hill and scrambled through the trees at the top, I never saw another soul. My place. Years later, my little brother told me he had found it too, all those years ago, and felt the same way. It made me feel warm, because in the end, magic is meant to share and he brought things back to life in my memory.

Someday, an orange 1970 Duster will pass me, going the other way. I'll hesitate just a moment, then crank the wheel hard and go after it.

If I can find it again, we could build ourselves a house there, Ghost.

My dream has no front door. It's impossible to say if it's big or small because it changes. I see a foyer with high ceilings and grassy places to lie down. We'll watch sunlight through stained glass, like it's television. When we go to the backyard to feed the fish, shy mermaids will abandon their sunbathing, slide off rocks to disappear beneath the surface. They'll leave behind a trail of sparking froth, and your lips will barely move as you count their bubbles.

Overhead, ship's sails will snap and rattle when the breeze comes up. We'll build secret rooms that we'll never find again. Strange animals will show up in the back yard, and I'll ask you if they live here with us and you'll laugh and say probably, so I better feed them.

There will be striped umbrellas and drooping palms. I see flowers everywhere, on trees and bushes. They change color by themselves, but always, always, stay pink. Casey Kasem will bring us all the hottest hits of all the summers there ever were, all the time.

We'll keep a big telescope for looking at the moon, and a giant kaleidoscope so we can talk to all the people we miss. At night, lights will do strange things in the sky. We'll fall asleep watching them.

You'll hold my hand and tell me the future, like a story.

Someday—when I see you again.

Bob Bickford

Love, Ghost

Dear Ghost,

    The dogs are asleep, squeezed together into the footwell beneath my desk.
    You walk in summer, through the shush of surf, footprints in the sand. I sit in winter and write you letters.
    This isn't actually much of an office. It's a disused hallway, a strange anachronism tacked onto the back of a very old house. There were no closets in these ancient houses; they used standing wardrobes like Narnia. At some point in the 1940s someone decided a hallway full of closets would set things right, so they built one onto the back. It's a place Alice would have understood—a hallway that leads no-place-at-all, made only of closets.
    The man who supervised the job, knocking out all those closets and cutting holes in the walls for an eclectic assortment of windows, is gone now. He was a good man. I can still see him and hear his voice.
    There's a big picture window, salvaged for free from a glass company up the street. It came from somebody's living room, and it used to look at somewhere else. Until recently, a tree grew right in front of it. They told me I shouldn't have a tree so close to the house, but a family of raccoons used it and they would sometimes pause halfway up to watch me. It made green curtains in the summer, so my space felt like a fort from when you were little. An ice storm took it down two years ago. I wanted to cry but couldn't. It was only a tree.
    When I look out the window tonight the Pacific Ocean washes up against the glass. It's the sea I was born in and will go back to someday.
    A dozen windows made in 1913, salvaged because they have stained glass insets, fill the other walls. Beautiful they are, and so leaky they need to be covered in plastic

in the winter or it gets as cold as sitting outside. Seventeen mismatched windows let in the sun and messy woods, where there were coat hangers and boxes and the dark.

The desk sat on a curb once, in the rain, waiting for the garbage truck. I stuffed it into the back of my ancient jeep and brought it home. I covered it in old varnish the color of fancy honey and stood it against a door that goes absolutely nowhere. The people who designed a hallway full of closets must have had a reason to include a door, but it's lost now. It got left alone because it would have meant a lot of trouble to tear it out. The chair came from the dump, and the stern woman in the fabric store told me the remnant I was buying was absolutely unsuitable for covering a chair, which made it perfect for a hallway of lost things.

An antique Packard key, a clock that will say 5:24 forever, a working 1938 Philco radio, the lovely ghosts of lovely dogs, a tiny image of Yankee Stadium, a map of 1940 Los Angeles. A very old fish tank full of minnows that were meant to be bait but swim safe. They pay me back with the sound of running water, which keeps me safe. Paintings made by someone who fell in love with Monet. Fragments and Letters, all of it.

A few nights ago, I was falling asleep and remembered a random incident that happened in Los Angeles, in 1982. It was a good story, but one I won't tell now. I'm blessed, or cursed, with vivid recollection and I recall the whole thing as clearly as if it happened an hour ago. It jolted me, realizing that every single one of the players is gone. I can still hear their voices, and in my reverie, they aren't even old yet. I suspect they didn't know their stories would have an ending.

I'm the last one left—when I go, there will be nobody left from that scene. Those voices and that story will disappear, at least from this side. I don't know if it matters, but it seems like enough reason to scribble.

Love, Ghost

You liked this hallway that goes nowhere. "Nowhere is still somewhere," you always said, and showed me your Wonderland smile.

Bob Bickford

Love, Ghost

Dear Ghost,

I've been walking the same set of train tracks for so long—since you were gone—I think of them as ours. It's where I talk to you.

You can't see the trains anymore, of course. The metal rails were pulled up about the time we were born. No creosote ties are left to smell oily these days when the summer sun gets hot. The line has been drifted over with dirt. Trees won't root on the cinders that lay just beneath the warm earth, and everything else grows different. Stands of purple loosestrife and wild parsnip go crazy, in a straight line as far as I can see.

The railbed is easy to find if you look—and I do.

Close to town, things have been dug up and built on over the years. The tracks dive deep, to run beneath things.

The last cars that rolled this way were pulled behind steam locomotives. All these years later, the ghost trains run through new construction, backyard trampolines, sidewalks, and swimming pool plantings. The part I usually walk on is a recreational path to the next town, but if you follow the line on a satellite map, you'll see farm lanes and bits of back road, a fence line or a path between fields and empty lots. People have used the dead remains, without knowing where the straight lines came from.

The woods are best. The aisle between trees holds a green-tinted silence that cools and heals me.

I met a very old man on the path, once. He seemed surprised that I knew about the tracks we stood on. He pointed out an ornamental hand pump in someone's side yard, painted white. He told me the locomotives paused on this spot to build steam before climbing the next grade. Hobos, overheated from a boxcar day in the sun, jumped off for a quick splash, a drink of fresh water, and a miser's bath from the pump. Whoever owns the house now has no idea their antique curio pump used to flow cold and sweet, that their yard was once oasis for the hot, the dirty, the tired, the thirsty.

I wonder if the house is blessed. I wonder if the people who live in it now fight less, worry less, dream sweeter, without knowing the shadows of dead strangers love them and say thank you.

A couple of hundred miles away, in Algonquin Park (Yosemite but without hot water), a canoe friend found a strange, straight bit of path that started in the middle of forest and ran along the edge of a lake. It started and then stopped for no reason, out in the middle of nowhere. It wasn't an animal trail. My friend wondered if I knew what it meant, since I like old puzzles.

I had an idea. Old maps tell stories—and yes, the mystery path is our tracks, still running west.

I follow the locomotive trail of steam tonight, on my evening walk, because it's where you walk, too. Your train runs here, and it's here you wait for me.

It's summer now. It's nice. I need to hurry just a little, because the sun goes down almost all at once, this time of year. I'm not exactly afraid of the trail in the dark, but the thing is—it could go anywhere. In places where time ripples, lost tends to stay lost.

A mile from home this evening, near the top of a trestle, a sofa sits just off the tracks, knee-deep in wild mint. A pretty sofa, covered with red and yellow flowers, by itself, just like so. The kind of sofa that invites a nap, with good lemonade and a good book and a good dog.

Of course, a sensible person would shake their head at some people using the woods as a dump—and keep walking. I'm talking about an imaginary sensible person because nobody linear would be walking this faint path at sunset in the first place. I'm not sensible, but I would point out to that person we're at the top of a steep embankment. Getting a sofa up would probably take four people, and it must be an eighth of a mile from any spot where you could unload it from a vehicle.

Somebody went to a lot of effort to put this sofa here. Something doesn't make sense.

Letters are written, you whisper. They wait to be read. When the shadows don't seem quite right, you know love has come to visit.

There's a nice view down the embankment. A creek at the bottom rushes white in the spring, but now it takes its time and rests here and there, in green pools. The sofa is actually quite clean, like it was never used much, and it hasn't been here long enough to get rained on. It's been arranged toward the last of the falling sun. I'd like to sit down, but at first, I don't. I know that you would, immediately, and that makes me smile.

If you were here, you'd point out white rabbit tracks, so I'd see at once and understand perfectly and stop wondering how the sofa got here. The world would get brighter and deeper.

You still make me sad and happy, Ghost, and most of all...

Sit down, you say, a little impatient. Talk to me. Tell me—everything.

So, I do. The cushions are soft, and they smell of red and yellow flowers. I wonder if I'll be able to kiss you, later.

The sunset is beautiful, and I'm not afraid when it gets dark.

Bob Bickford

Dear Ghost,

You told me I needed to surrender. You said it might be the most important thing I ever learned.
"Surrender doesn't mean giving up," you said.
You liked to tell me incomprehensible things once I drifted too close to slumber to turn back. If I had questions, I had no way to ask them except in dreams.
"The sooner you surrender," you whispered, "the sooner you'll be able to fall asleep. Trust me."
I did trust you. I still do.
One night, I walked alone across a railway trestle. I was seventeen.
The bridge made a slightly risky shortcut that shaved a few minutes from the walk home. The tracks ran through a grassy, woodsy strip of map that divided end of city and the beginning of our small town. The trestle crossed a river, then a road. On the far side, a grassy embankment rose to meet the railbed, just far enough away to mean running if a train came. It wasn't a thing to try during winter, or in the rain.
Look along the track both ways and squint, listen for a distant horn, then go-go-go.
I heard kids used to jump off in the middle—for fun—into the river. They must have been pioneer kids, made of stern stuff, because I never knew anyone who did it. My dad walked about eighty miles to school with holes in his shoes, so it sounded like something his generation would have enjoyed. We modern kids weren't that crazy. It reassured us though, knowing if a train rolled up, we could just use the long-ago-kids' escape route. We could jump.
At seventeen, a warm July midnight, I walked alone across the railway trestle.
I had left behind a street party, a clowder of friends, loud music, noisy mufflers, and a considerable number of

emptied bottles of Molson Golden pale ale. My car sat at home in the driveway that night. Maybe my dad had taken the keys for some offense, or maybe a guardian angel killed the battery. I don't remember.

Vague recollection surfaces, some trouble with another group, trouble that had grown into pushing and threats, but not quite resolved. The party began to feel stupid. I hadn't yet developed the recklessness that defined me later, so I decided to abandon the impending fight and go home by myself on foot. At some point under the streetlights, it occurred to me that I had put myself at risk by separating from my pack. Trouble might have spotted me alone and followed. I didn't much care.

I've never done well in a tribe. I've always preferred my chances alone.

After a couple of miles, looking back over my shoulder into the dark, imagining footsteps, I reached the trestle. Beer said that it presented a good opportunity to lose any hostile shadows, since nobody would follow me across the river in the dark. I left the road, stepped onto the tracks, and started across. The moon and stars gave just enough light to polish the rails. A slow, careful rhythm kept my feet on the ties without twisting an ankle. It made a ridiculous risk.

Seventeen is the hardest age, I think. Adulthood and a carefully planned future never weigh as heavy as they do at seventeen.

After I turned twenty, I was pretty sure I wouldn't be a doctor. Twenty-five, and I knew I wasn't going to play baseball for a living, hear my latest release on the radio, or marry a runway model. At thirty, I felt certain I would never drive a brand-new BMW off the showroom floor, never display its keys on a bar top.

By my fortieth birthday, I cut my own grass and washed my own dishes and didn't know why I had ever wanted any of those things.

At seventeen, though, I believed I should do all of it. I didn't know any better. You were an ocean away, Ghost, busy being sixteen. I had barely imagined or remembered you yet. The world maybe weighed too much to let me see a railway trestle in the dark as a bad idea.

I stopped at the mid-point of the bridge to look at the river, glinting dark below me. I might have been there for a while because I was still drunk and my thoughts probably moved slowly. At some point, I realized the rails at my feet were lit brighter than the moon could account for. The diesel air horn sounded at the same moment I comprehended the single headlight. Paralysis held me for an agonizing second, then I turned and ran.

The trestle vibrated beneath me. A single misstep, one foot between the wooden ties, and I would have been finished. Somehow, I didn't falter. The railing ended, so even in the dark I knew I had reached the point where the grassy slope rose from the roadway to meet the tracks. I didn't dare look back over my shoulder. I zigged to the right and jumped.

The train might not have been as close as I imagined. The ground was definitely nowhere near as close as I calculated. I had jumped too soon. I'm not sure how far I dropped, but if I had a ripcord, I could have pulled it on the way down. When I landed, the impact compressed my guts and knocked the air from my lungs. I rolled down the slope and came to rest, face up.

Far above me, the train rumbled past, wheels knocking and hissing, steel on steel. Then everything got quiet.

I understood that I was hurt, maybe seriously. I spent my summers lifeguarding and had trained for spinal injuries. I knew I shouldn't move. My breathing started again and steadied by degrees. I guessed nobody would find me before morning.

On my back, I watched the night sky. The moon had gone to a horizon I couldn't see, getting ready for morning, but the stars still tracked across the black. If you watch stars long enough, they change colors and move on their own. Passing night creatures rustled, noted my presence, and paused, then went about their business. In my helplessness, I became one of them. The wind whispered in the grass and made the dark trees shift overhead.

Just out of my sight, the river moved. All at once, I understood that all the sunny brooks and underground streams, the lakes and oceans and rainstorms, were connected as a simple expression of the eternal. The living and the dead flow, all part of the same story. All water is the same water.

The dirt I lay on cradled and soothed me. The earth is mother, soft and true. It was the least alone I've ever been. The memory comforts me, even today.

That's when you came, Ghost. I hadn't seen you since we were little. You moved across the grass with your usual grace, a shadow glowing a little lighter than the rest of the night, lit from inside. I saw you and heard you and felt you, decades before I met you again in real life.

You held your hair back, bent over me, and laughed, delighted. "What are you doing here?"

"I fell," I said. "Or jumped. I'm not sure. Are you real?"

Your smile faded. You tilted your head, considering. "Does it matter?"

I decided it didn't, not really. You laughed again, like chimes.

"Very good," you said. "This is surrender. Now you know. Surrender matters more than anything. It doesn't mean giving up, though. Let's go."

I took the hand you held out, and you helped me up. You slipped one arm around my waist and started me walking. For a shadow, you felt strong and warm. You felt like a missing piece, back in place.

"You'll be okay," you said. "I think your chances of being a professional ballet dancer are probably finished, though."

"Add that to the list," I said.

Headlights spread across the road just as we reached the shoulder, and in their light, you were gone. The cop looked like my father. He put me in the back seat, said some incomprehensible things into his radio. Then he turned, one arm across the back of the seat. He told me he was too busy with other calls to figure out what I was doing there and why he should arrest me. He drove me home. When I got out, he made me promise not to go out again that night.

I think he was kind and decent, so I kept my promise. As it happened, I didn't leave the house for a week. Once the beer wore off, I could barely get out of bed. When I had to, I walked slowly to the bathroom, bent over.

I'm not too far away from being an old man now, and my back has hurt most days since then. The bridge has stayed with me, a whole lifetime. Last year, I sat across from my doctor while she looked at x-ray images.

"I dropped off a bridge when I was a kid," I told her. "Long time ago. Probably fell further than you'd believe."

She nodded, not really interested, and recommended exercises instead of surgery. I had figured the same thing, most of my life. I nodded, not really interested either.

Not so long ago, I asked you if you had really been there that night. You smiled and didn't answer my question. You almost never did.

I don't mind the ache in my back. For the most part, I don't even notice it. When I do, it reminds me of a summer night, that the earth is mother, and that water is eternal. It reminds me to surrender.

It reminds me of you.

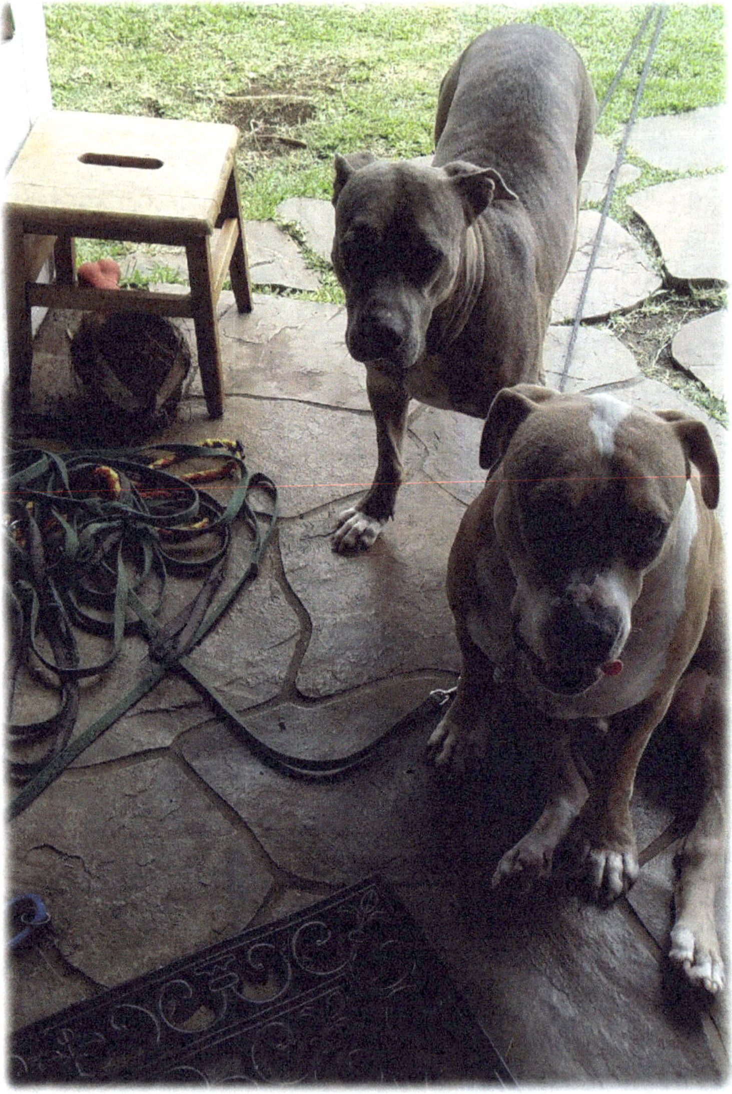

Dear Ghost,

You asked me once what I believed in.
I said I believed in dragons. They follow some people. I told you I believed in grace, and that crayons with funny names—"cornflower" and "periwinkle" and "magenta"—color truest. That was all I could think of.
You nodded, like I made perfect sense, without looking up. You sorted your collection of pebbles and bright glass, seashells and bird skulls and Polaroid photographs. I knew the changing patterns told you something—the truth maybe, or the future. You paused your sifting and held out a hand, palm up.
"Give me a moment of your life you don't want," you said. "I'll put it somewhere you won't have to see it anymore."
That was easy, since I had a lot of them. I thought about it, and gave you:
A fancy L.A club, full of empty people, one in the morning, a rich woman paying the tab. I'm so drunk on White Russians I can barely stay pointed northeast. The woman looks across the table and shows me a brilliant smile, because she knows I know I'm not enough and I don't belong here and we both saw the valet smirk when I got out of the car. I hate myself, and she breathes that in deep, like cocaine.
"Please don't start a fight with anyone here," she says. "This isn't that kind of place."
My kind of place, she means. She casts eyes around the room and hopes I really will start a fight, with anyone at all.

I gave you that moment, Ghost. You closed your hand and found a deep pocket in your robe. The sunshine outside the sliding glass door flickered for a moment, then steadied and turned bright. A part of me didn't hurt, anymore. You healed me, somehow.

"Now give me a moment to keep," you said. "One I can take out to look at when you're not here."

I reached for a moment I wouldn't trade for anything, a single moment that defined me, one I'd want scattered with my ashes. I couldn't come up with anything. I hadn't lived that kind of life. You read me while your black eyes moved through all the colors, all the pages of all my days.

"You know the one I want," you said. "Right?"

"Coffee with honey," I answered, like that made any sense, and you nodded.

It's about six in the morning, I think. I don't have a watch. I'm sitting on a cement wall. The last of my dollar bills are gone, and the ocean is gray, as far as I can see. The sand is cold, dimpled by yesterday's beach people. My jean jacket isn't enough, but I've been colder than this.

I haven't seen the sun come up over these waters since I was little. I think about the people I've lost, since then. I've been gone a long time.

This is the Pacific, so it gets day for a while before yellow and orange light creeps over the soft old mountains behind me and tumbles down into the water. The morning goes from gray to blue. Far out in the channel, islands turn pink in the thin light. I know sea lions are stirring and looking at the dawn like it's the first time.

There's going to be an art show later. A hippie-looking woman moves along the boardwalk, setting up easels. She catches me watching and crooks a finger at me— come here. I can't think of any reason I shouldn't, so I find my feet. My legs ache a little, with long walking and the chill. The woman wears a loose skirt, a long braid, and sandals. Her feet are lean and elegant. She bends as I

Love, Ghost

approach and pours coffee from a thermos into a paper cup.

"This is all you need," she says.

She turns and presses the cup into my hands. The coffee is fragrant, and the cup is printed with red and yellow flowers. Her fingers are warm. I realize it's been a long time since anyone touched me.

She seems like a strange woman, strangely beautiful and strangely familiar, even though I've never seen her before. I start to thank her, but she doesn't want to talk. She smiles, a smile that could mean anything at all, and shoos me away. I return to my low cement wall and my backpack, find my lighter and my crumpled pack of Kool Lights. The coffee is hot, black, and sweet. It takes a second to realize it tastes of honey, not sugar.

A glance at the woman, but she has her back to me now, busy with her day.

Drinking my coffee, I think the woman is right. I don't need anything else. It's going to be hot later. The sea lions are awake. Anything might happen and probably will.

You held out your hand, so I gave you that moment to keep, too. You put it somewhere you could find it when you missed me, then went back to arranging your seashells. You said nothing else.

I told you once I believe in dragons, Ghost—but I also told you I believe in grace, and that crayons with funny names—"cerulean" and "indigo" and "carnation"—color truest. I believe in love, without the slightest idea of what that means.

You walk beside a river of time these days. I wonder if your footprints go back to find me all those years ago. I think about red and yellow flowers, and I wonder if you once poured me a cup.

"Thanks for the coffee," I say, in case you can hear me.

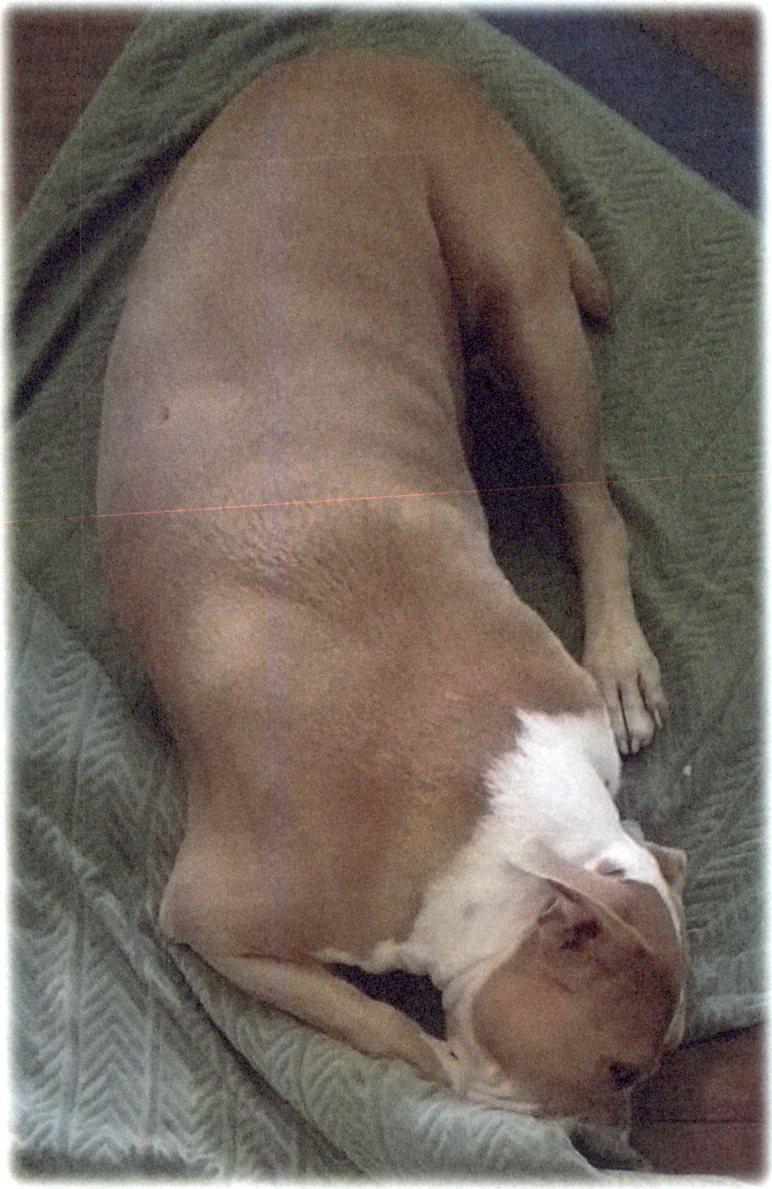

Dear Ghost,

Once, I knew a girl who saved all my letters in a place where nobody would find them. She folded and slid them into the sleeve of a David Bowie album: Scary Monsters (and Super Creeps). It made a safe place her mom would never look.

We spent all day together, most days, but we had a ten o'clock curfew on weeknights. Her parents were generous, but the deadline stayed stern and unmovable. End-of-day included the telephone on the kitchen wall. At one minute past ten, I kissed the young woman good night, then walked down her dark front walk and out to the subway, back to whatever address I slept at that month.

Without her, the night-city seemed suddenly lonely, the towers tall, the lights cold.

I wrote her letters, against the dark. I sat on the bed in my rooming house, shuffled Supertramp on my small record player, and tried to tell her everything. The next night, she sat on her bed on the other side of town and read what I wrote, then tucked the pages into the album sleeve. Across the city, I wrote the next one while she read. It made a way to talk, to be together when we were apart, which is what letters do if they're any good.

Eventually, she broke my heart. It's only now, all these years later, that I realize I broke her heart, too. Maybe I did it first. She went away. I saw her one May morning in 1982, as I walked on Avenue Road in Toronto. She passed by in a blue car, going the other way. She wore sunglasses and didn't turn her head, but I imagine she spotted me. I got on a Greyhound bus not long after that, and I never saw her again.

I'm glad I didn't know the blue car and sunglasses was the last time. There are some things a heart can't know, or the breaking would be too much. Sometimes, I wonder what happened to my letters.

My mom taught me how to write letters before any of that. Six years old, and every Sunday afternoon found me sitting at our dining room table in small-town Kansas. I had a piece of lined paper. I also had a yellow pencil, never quite sharp enough, because my mom whittled points with a kitchen knife instead of using a sharpener.

I had to write a weekly letter to a woman I never met. She lived in a far-off state, North Carolina. I addressed her as "Granny", although she was some sort of distant relative and not quite my grandmother. The letter writing commenced after lunch and lasted until done, regardless of how long it took. Between morning church and afternoon letter, every summer Sunday balanced on the edge of complete waste.

The letter formula didn't vary. Three paragraphs about my week's events, three sentences each, simple and compound mixed in a way that pleased my mom's eye. She expected symmetry and balance, with perfect grammar a given.

The kicker was that the letter had to be interesting. If my mom read the finished letter and decided it was boring, it meant starting again. Lies were also considered cheating. The stories had to be both compelling and sincere. Finding topics and events in my six-year-old life that would engage an old woman in another state meant chewing the end of my pencil and digging deep.

Dear Granny,
We got a new brown-and-white dog. The first day, he threw up on the living room rug. His name is Smokey.

My dad put a new swimming pool in the back yard and filled it with the garden hose, but nobody goes in. The water is too cold to swim. He says he doesn't know why he bothers, and my mom laughs at him when he's not looking.

I climbed the tree in the front yard. At the very top, I can look down and see two balls and a Frisbee on our roof. This is why I like summer.

Love, Bobby

When I'm asked, I always say if you can write a letter to Granny, you can write any damn thing you want to. You can write magic spells. Letters, taught to me by my young mother in a dining room in Halstead, Kansas when I was six. A sunny table, lined paper, a yellow pencil sharpened with a knife. Scratch on paper, look out the window, sigh. Done, Mom checks spelling and grammar. Fold it neatly into envelope, lick American flag stamp, then you're free. Go outside to play. Magic.

Now I write letters to you, Ghost. My life (and love) depends on it. You sit in the sun, faraway, and eat an orange while you read them.

When it all becomes play, when love and need are one, when I want to keep going, the letters come to life. Colored powders, magic—tinted smoke and sparkles and music. Mix and stir, study alchemy, check my watch, count the years of my life and despair there won't be enough of them to figure it all out.

I want to tell you everything. I won't pull it off, but it's important to try.

Love, Ghost

That isn't the point of this, though. You asked me once what I would have done with my life if I could have done anything with my life. I told you I would have found you. That made you laugh, but it was true. I got my dream-come-true, my heart's desire, at least for a little while.

"Maybe for forever," you whisper. "We'll see when we get there."

All the letters of my life were meant for you. Given a do-over, I would have caused less hurt and worried less. I would have made a few left turns in places where I went right, but the teenaged beers, the Greyhound stations at midnights, the mad crushes who kissed someone else, the Styrofoam cups of Burger King coffee, the dirty hotels, the broken hearts, the junky old cars with big engines, the girls who made me laugh, the brilliant beach days with two bucks in my pocket, are what mattered.

I write you those eternal things in letters. Dying's not so hard, when it's not for keeps. Finding you is exactly how I would spend my life again, given a second chance. Those small things along the way are what I treasure, and what I'll remember. The true love and monsters. The wasted time, the warm mornings in strange places, are what we take with us when we go.

Our beautiful, messy lives, dipped in amber.

Bob Bickford

Love, Ghost

Dear Ghost,

One afternoon, I sat beside you while you read a letter. When you finished, you carefully folded the single sheet of paper back into its envelope. Neither of us spoke. I knew better than to ask. You might tell me one day, or not. The paper-and-ink stained your heart, not mine. I think the ability to keep quiet is one of the things that let me get close to you.

A single drop of water glistened on your bare knee. A moment passed before I recognized the teardrop for what it was. It shone, a prism for skin the exact color of honey. You sat quietly, with your head bowed. I remember the textures of you. I could smell the swimming pool on your skin, the sun in your hair. I wanted to touch you, but I didn't. I wanted to cry with you, but I had forgotten how.

I thought about Alice, swimming in an ocean of her own tears.

I did what I could. I only work in awkward blurts. I took both your hands and reminded you that we were eleven, once. Come with me, I told you, to a different afternoon.

Sting-Rays, canted over jaunty on kickstands, wait for us. My friend has a green Krate, a Pea Picker with the small front wheel and a sissy bar. Mine is basic, dark gold with red-stripe tires. Tie my towel, one of the threadbare ones my mom keeps on a shelf in the laundry room, around my banana seat, then we're off.

Down the driveway, bump over the curb, coast past the tire store and the plumbing-supply place. We're down to the river. In town, the water runs dark beneath cement bridges and laps the brick base of a textile mill that's been closed and haunted for years. That river keeps secrets, has seen bad things. It's grown-up water: all the things that are coming.

Pedal hard. Chains rattle as the asphalt beneath our tires changes to gravel at the edge of town. Glasgow Road follows the river through Dick's Dam Park. The stream is different here: truer, and ours. Beneath the trees, the water runs shallow enough in places to see bottom rocks beneath the sparkles. Our spot is deeper, a pool carved out where the course nearly stops as it bends and turns back on itself.

Other kids are already there. Drop the bikes on grass, t-shirts floating down. Run.

The fearless kids climb the trees, drop from high branches into the dark pool. I'm not that brave. I tell myself I would climb if I wanted to, but I like jumping from the bank more. I know I'm not heroic. Even the four-foot drop from the bank scares me.

You told me later that not being a fearless kid, but doing the things I did anyway, made me the bravest of all. You said a lifetime of being afraid is why I walk dark streets nobody else will, and why I'm drawn to protect the littlest creatures. I loved you for that. I wanted it to be true.

The water shocks, then feels cool and silky. Sunlight turns the underwater green. Surface to wipe my face, look up at leaf-dapple. This is pure goodness, and nobody made it. Nobody drew it up on architect paper, nobody scraped it out with bulldozers. This is how the world is supposed to be. The quietest places are the miracles closest to where we came from, the promises we'll go back to.

I've spent most of my life forgetting that, Ghost. The quiet places were always at your center. Maybe that's why people thought you strange.

Our shouting and splashing stops when someone spots the snake. Against the far bank, a tell-tale ripple. There's a mad scramble, everyone out of the river. I stay where I am, tread water and imagine I feel her undulations, marvel that I share this water and this world with such a creature. She isn't interested in us, carries on with her business and is lost to sight at the river bend. Not all the scary things want to hurt you.

Towel off and ride back. Inside the drugstore I check my pocket. My shorts stay a little bit wet from the river, but I still have the quarter I brought from home. Enough for an ice cream cone and an Almond Joy. A parking lot we know is always empty because the store is closed, so it works as a speedway. Round and round, the course marked by sticks and rocks. The Krate is lighter than my classic Sting-Ray, but I wouldn't trade. My friend doesn't mind beating me every time.

At his house, there will be hamburgers and corn on the cob for dinner, and I'm allowed to sleep over. We ride to my house for my pajamas and toothbrush on the edge of darkness—come straight back—and my house looks the same, like my day on the river never happened. It's me that's different.

"I want to stay here," you murmured.

I got up then, went inside and brought you back an orange. It was what I had for you, talismans against your sadness, an orange and a different afternoon. You peeled the fruit in one curl, the way you always did, like it was no big deal. You gave me a segment and I reminded myself to remember the way it tasted. The oranges you gave me were always the sweetest.

"What's next?" you asked.

We ride back to my friend's house and his mom lets us drink a little grape soda with television. His dad never says much. He's drinking beer, Carling Black Label, in a brown bottle. I pretend my soda is beer. I can't wait until I'm old enough to drink all the beer I want. I don't know that's a sad wish I'll be granted.

Upstairs, the sheets are clean, but they don't smell like my house. The streetlight shadows on the ceiling are different. That's okay—I'm safe. Learning how to be safe in strange places is another wish I'll be granted.

I fall asleep thinking about the river.

We floated back from that long-ago afternoon. Your shoulders changed, and you shifted a little to slip one arm around me. The teardrop had gone to wherever teardrops go, but I could still see the spot on your bare knee. I imagine it lingers, wherever you are now.

When I was five, they told me that a Bassett hound named Barney who lived across the street had died. He was my sad-faced friend. I didn't understand because I had seen him in his yard that morning, hunting for something in the grass.

In grade eight, I had a desperate crush on a girl with hair so blonde it was nearly white. On an overnight school trip to a capital city, I sat two rows behind her on the yellow bus and watched her kiss a boy—for four hours. I heard my heart crack whenever the bus went over bumps.

I've gone swimming in your river of tears, Ghost.

I never got as wet as I did that afternoon, though, in that one perfect teardrop on your knee. I told you a river story while it evaporated into the sky that birthed it, back to the rainclouds, back to the rivers.

Your single tear, a cool, green place to swim. At long last, I leave my Sting-Ray on the bank, climb the tree to the highest branch, and drop. You, forever.

Bob Bickford

Dear Ghost,

I'm not sure why three in the morning is my goodbye time. It's just how things turn out. I never walk away on autumn afternoons, in golden sunshine, kicking red leaves like a 1970s love story. I always do my stepping out from beneath fluorescent lights, when the whole world is asleep. My leaving involves empty stretches of pavement, dying moths, a faint threat of frost on cold night air, the neon buzz from a Waffle House sign.

My goodbyes usually get said to people who are already gone, heard by nobody at all.

The November buses out of Toronto run all night. It's 1982, and Greyhound doesn't care what time it is. Whenever I'm ready to leave, the dog is ready to run. On Bay Street, the bus station waits for me. I pull open the heavy glass door and go inside.

I'm tired. I only have a single knapsack, not much gear to cross into the unknown, but it holds all I want to take with me. It's gotten heavier over the last couple hours. I stopped last night for a late dinner and I've been moving south ever since, a good-bye-to-this-city walk.

There's a Mexican restaurant a few miles north on Yonge Street, just past Eglinton Avenue. It opened a couple years ago, maybe the first place north of the border to offer menudo and carnitas. My mom went to high school in San Antonio and fell in love with poblanos, jalapeños, guajillos, and habaneros. She served us canned tamales for lunch or baked enchiladas for dinner when she was in a happy mood. She substituted mounds of raw onion when we lived in places that had never heard of hot peppers. She figured onions did the same thing, more or less, if you closed your eyes.

The Toronto Star review said the new chef came from India. Being from New Delhi didn't mean he had never been to Mexico, my mom said. She figured he had probably learned to cook on dusty streets, taught by women with emotionless faces and black eyes. He had likely sipped Modelo, watched the sun slip behind the Sierra Madre de Chiapas, and felt he was home.

"Imagine a real Mexican restaurant this far north," my mom said. "Toronto is getting so cosmopolitan. We might as well be living in Paris, France."

She loved France, too. She kept a little jar on her bedside table, filled with pebbles she had collected from the beach at Nice.

I loved the idea of Mexico, its sun and colors and warm, strange ways. I loved a pepper-burn in my mouth as much as my mom did. It was our thing. Excited, we made plans to go to the new restaurant on my next birthday. She figured it would be worth waiting—give the chef a couple months to get the kinks worked out. She looked happy and young and pretty, thinking about it. She was always young and pretty, but only happy sometimes.

"It's been so long since I had real food," she sighed. "I can't wait."

She didn't live until my birthday, so we didn't go. That's just the way stories go, sometimes.

Here in 1982, I've passed the restaurant hundreds of times but never gone inside. The place feels haunted to me, a memorial to shock and loss. The sign always makes me a little angry, like it's been lit up to remind me. I'm sure the chef mixes cobwebs and dust into his aguachile, and the tequila tastes of tears.

Tonight, my last night here, I follow impulse inside. I only have a thin sheaf of twenties to take me west, so I'm spending money I really don't have. It's not my birthday, but it's a good-bye I owe, and a last chance to say it.

Love, Ghost

I'm just a scruffy young guy, not much more than a kid. The woman inside looks doubtful but wheels away. I follow her full skirt and fancy sandals to a table. Couples sit across candles from each other, look up from each other's faces as I pass. My server has lipstick that shines bright red, even in the gloom. I try to explain to her that I might not belong here, with these evening-dressed people, but I'm your oldest, your best, your most faithful customer. I've been waiting to eat here since before you opened. She nods, leaves a menu, and doesn't care.

Everything on the list seems familiar and painful. I can't eat any of it, so I order a half-pitcher of Sangria. The shadow of my mom shakes her head and says that's the last thing I need. Her ghost stands up and leaves the table. I drink my drinks, down to melted ice, alone. The wine and citrus must be watered down, because I don't feel a thing.

Then I walk this city a last time, all the way south. From a doorway, Springsteen sings about tramps like us. Somewhere along the way, the clock moves past midnight and into the next day.

The old station on Bay Street has seen its best days. Until last year, the grand staircase led up to a luncheonette where nobody ate. Phantoms sat unmoving at the dirty counter, nursing the same cup of coffee, sipping sweeteners from paper-bag bottles. Now, sawhorses guard the top.

Drivers on break shuffle through the fluorescent flickers, holding on to Styrofoam cups. A khaki man with a thousand keys hung from his back pocket pushes a dry mop, an eternal tour of the station floor. The sleeping forms on plastic benches have always been here, never moved. The man behind the ticket glass doesn't look at me. Los Angeles is a long way, with a lot of changes. His lips move as he figures out the ticket.

"Seventy-five-fifty," he says.

I do a quick figure. That's going to leave me about seventeen bucks to cross the country, with likely nothing left when I get there. I'm not worried.

"You have to get off in Buffalo," he says. "Be sure to get your luggage from underneath. You have to take your bags through customs yourself."

Outside, the cold air reeks of diesel. The driver stands by the bus door, collecting tickets. He looks through me when I thank him. I'm already fading from here, going invisible, and that makes me strangely happy.

The clutch chatters as the big bus lurches a wide right onto Bay Street. The Gardiner Expressway is a dark river. We pick up speed, headed for Route 66.

Roll through New York, the endlessness of Ohio and Indiana. The dirty arch over St. Louis means the east is behind me. The Mississippi River doesn't look like much, but a million people have gazed at it and dreamed, so it matters in some deep way. By Oklahoma City, November will start to feel a little warmer.

Cadillac Ranch outside Amarillo is worth the trip by itself, a line of DeVilles nose-down in the dirt, tailfins raised to the sky. Albuquerque reminds me of the Mexican restaurant and makes me sad again. There's a little snow in Kingman, Arizona. The air is western warm, so it's just decoration. The palm trees start in San Berdoo. From there we roll into Los Angeles like it's downhill. Cloverleaf off the freeway, and I'm home.

A three-day ride.

Downtown is a literal war zone, but it's L.A. It's where my heart lives, so the beach isn't that far away. I need a shower. I like to be clean, and there's no place cleaner than the Pacific Ocean. The western sea is always a little cold, so November won't make much difference. The sun is gold, and the air is softer and sweeter than anywhere else in the world. Forget what you've heard—L.A smells wonderful.

Love, Ghost

No matter what else happens, it's all an adventure and it's all going to be okay.

You were my ghost before you were a ghost, Ghost. I don't know your name yet, or what you look like, but I'll sit on the sand, look west, and dream about you. It's all just starting.

Nothing lasts forever—except maybe you.

It's a good thing to remember sometimes, now I'm getting old. Don't cling to the safety of a bus station at three-ayem. Heaven means a long stretch of Route 66 before you get there, a three-day ride that smells like cold and diesel. If you only have seventeen bucks in your pocket, you get on the damn bus anyway. Under grimy fluorescent lights, you stand in nighttime November and believe in California, no matter what.

Chances are, somebody you love will be waiting on the west coast, ready to take you out for Mexican food.

Bob Bickford

Love, Ghost

Dear Ghost,

My dad told me once, when I was young, that life is nothing but a long series of good-byes.

Other people have said the same thing in nearly the same words, but my dad didn't say it like Billy Joel song lyrics. He said it like it was the only thing he'd ever really learned, the only thing he trusted.

We sat across from each other, drinking rye-and-ginger, having a rare, civilized discussion. As a teenager, I had decided it was mostly better not to talk to talk to him. This truce seemed awkward and a little bit sweet, so I remember that drink and what he said. I remember the room, the cigarettes and ice cubes, the smell of fortified ginger ale.

Life is nothing but a long series of good-byes.

Years later, he got wheeled onto a hospital patio to feel the late June sun on his face. I tried not to watch his hands shake on the blanket in his lap. He told me not to waste an afternoon in such a place, that summers were too short and he would see me the next day. I didn't hold his trembling hands or kiss his cheek because that wasn't our way. As I walked across the wide lawns to my truck, I felt his eyes and his goodbye. I didn't turn around to go back or try to stop my absolute certainty that we would never speak again. As it turned out, we never did.

A child falls asleep watching teevee. Dead weight up the stairs to bed, head heavy on shoulder. It's the last time. The very next day they've grown too big to carry any more. Nobody decides, and nobody knows how the last time happens. It's just so.

Every day, we meet familiar things for the last time. We will never go back to a hundred places we love. We smile absently and thank grocery store cashiers we'll never see again. We're tired of Cheerios, so we switch cereals. We don't know we've bought our last box, eaten our last bowl, will never taste them again. The landmarks of our lives are torn down and replaced with landmarks for other people, the things they'll remember.

Strangers pass by, into the rest of their lives and their own endings. A series of goodbyes, the way it should be.

The Askew is a beach. We leave footprints in sand, not cement. The tide comes in, the surf washes them away. There will be other people's footprints later, and there's something lovely and comforting in that. We leave behind all the things we love, for them.

You crouch to write with a finger in the wet sand, Ghost. As we walk on, I look back over my shoulder at what you've scribbled in the foam.

"You're going to love this place."

Life is nothing but a long series of good-byes.

I remember you, and a swimming pool at night. We sat on the cement apron, hips and shoulders not quite brushing, watching the plumeria trees move their branches in the dark. We didn't say much. Water gurgled in the gutters and did our talking for us. There may have been fireflies. If phantoms moved across the grass toward us, I couldn't see them.

I told you about a glass of rye-and-ginger with my dad, and what he told me. When I was done, you didn't say anything. You walked every day through a part of forever that's uncomfortable. You knew those forever places better than me.

"Amtraks aren't all the same," you finally said. "It's okay."

You had your Alice ways, and you said your Alice-things that made no sense at first. Those things moved on their own into perfect sense, if they found someone willing to watch the dark and wait. I've always stayed willing, so I listened to the lap of swimming pool and followed a small plane blinking its way across the sky, east to west.

Life is nothing but a long series of good-byes.

In 1983, I took the Pacific Surfliner from San Luis Obispo to San Diego. A young woman came with me. We ate dinner on the way south. When I was little, the dining car meant uniformed conductors, china plates, and heavy silverware. Now the conductor's uniform still looked splendid, but he served linoleum floors and wrapped sandwiches and warm cans of Henry Weinhard's beer. I didn't mind. We had a good time, while the sun setting into the Pacific Ocean made that disposable dinner romantic as could be.

It was dark when the train paused in Los Angeles. The young woman got off to catch a flight headed east. I planned to follow her in a few weeks. We would only be apart for a little while. I helped with her bags. On the platform, she said she needed to talk to me. It seemed strange, since we had been talking for the last three hours. I guess I knew. I guess she didn't have to say anything.

She turned the watch on her wrist and didn't look at me. She told me that life is a series of goodbyes, and this was one of them. She had decided. She carried the burden of that impending parting all the way south, through the laughter and sandwiches and beer. I felt bad, for her awkwardness and discomfort. Feeling bad for me would come later. I got back on the train. She didn't kiss me. On the top step, I looked back and saw the relief on her face.

I watched for her on the platform as the train slid out, but she had already gone.

A lot of cans of beer was all I could think of, but the conductor told me it was too late to serve me even one. I could still buy a sandwich or a bag of potato chips, he said, but the bar was closed. I looked out the window and waited for the train to get to nowhere. Nobody waited for me in

San Diego, and I never flew east. Part of me still rides that train.

"You were never meant to fly east," you murmured. "East isn't your nature."

I thought about that, Alice-ghost. All at once I understood that I would never have reached a night-time swimming pool, and you, without taking that train. The Pacific Surfliner hurt, but our trains take us where we're going, if we can read the ticket. You healed me, the way you often do.

You were my station, Ghost. (You still are.) You waited for me in San Diego. I can live with you staying invisible, for now.

"You're right—Amtraks aren't all the same," I said. "Thank you."

"You're welcome," you said.

Life is nothing but a long series of good-byes.

Bob Bickford

Love, Ghost

Dear Ghost,

I miss you.

Bob Bickford

Love, Ghost

Dear Ghost,

One day, I'll get off the bus in the Askew. The brakes will squeal long before the big Greyhound shudders to a stop. The driver will hiss the front door open and look back up the aisle at me, waiting. It will be nighttime outside, still warm, because it's always a warm evening in the Askew. There will be flickering torches and the smell of flowers that only bloom in the dark. Beyond the firelit beach, the ocean will spread out, vast and black. The moon is the only familiar thing because it's always the same moon.

Bank accounts, beliefs about world order, and real estate holdings don't help here. Sexual conquests, promotions, alliances, vodka martinis, and gym memberships mean nothing. Those things remembered from being little—the taste of popsicles and pool water, the shadows that crawl across bedroom ceilings at night—might help a lot.

For all its strangeness, the Askew is a place we know. It's a song we remember, though we've forgotten the words. I lost you once, Ghost, when we were little. For a while, I didn't remember you.

When I was six, the prettiest girl I had ever seen sat at the very front desk in our classroom. There were girls with more flash, I guess. The Davis twins wore matching dresses and barrettes every day and laughed loudly. Other girls owned lighter hair or richer fathers. Not one of them stayed neat and quiet and smart like the girl in the front row, though. None of them had upturned noses or sat just so, with ankles crossed. They weren't just about perfect, like her.

I spent the school year seated several rows behind that girl, invisible. I drifted to sleep every night saving her from monsters and bank robbers. I flew her anywhere she wanted to go, in my biplane.

Once, after springtime recess, the school secretary came to the classroom door for me. I followed her to the office, frightened by the formality. The principal presented a message from my mom. She was serving on a committee with the girl's minister father—in hindsight likely something to do with starving people or the Vietnam war—and wouldn't make it home for lunch. He had offered to let me walk with the perfect girl to her house and eat there.

I nodded. I didn't even know our parents knew each other. I thought I must be dreaming.

The whole day became sweetly unreal. I drifted weightlessly back up the hall to my classroom, the apparition of a small boy in Keds and a green baseball cap, to wait for the noon bell. I'm not sure how I told the perfect girl about our date. Painfully shy, it seems likely that I said nothing and simply followed her home at a distance. No doubt her mother waited on the front veranda, unaware her daughter and I had never been introduced.

I remember sunshine, printed fabrics, and a ticking clock. The rectory, if they called it that, was as quiet and gracious as the mother. The perfect girl and I sat across the table from each other and got served chicken noodle soup, a cheese sandwich grilled in real butter, a glass of fresh, cold milk—all my favorites, as if they knew what I loved. If I were served lunch on my birthday in paradise, I would have asked for that menu. The sense of unreality increased.

She didn't speak to me. I didn't need her to.

Lunch at our house meant cacophony, with my mom hipshot at the counter, spreading peanut butter with the littlest toddler tucked into her waist. Small, lovely, harried by too many small children, she stayed modern and independent before there was such a thing. Cooking dinner for an army was bad enough—she wouldn't turn the

Love, Ghost

goddamned stove on at lunchtime, too. I hated peanut butter, and still do. Today, I wouldn't drink powdered milk at gunpoint. Our three dogs usually turned up at the lunch hour to eat sandwiches beneath the table, slipped to them when nobody was looking. Someone always spilled their glass of Tang across the linoleum tabletop. Someone else always cried.

For one day only, I had grilled cheese, chicken noodle, and thou.

All these years and all these miles later, I have never had a better meal. I ate a steak once on the top floor of a skyscraper, watching city lights spread out to make stars below the stars above. It came with wine, vegetables that were strangely charred, and cost more than I made in a whole day. That steak wasn't as good as chicken noodle and grilled cheese on a May noon hour in Kansas. Not even close.

When we were done, the perfect girl licked a milk mustache from her lip and spoke to me. I don't remember what she said, but I remember the moment like I'm there now. It remains a singularly wonderful instant, a light that has shone sweet possibility on the rest of my life.

So, I know a little about heaven.

At twenty-one, I had an accidental meeting and fell into the perfect job. All I had to do was hang around and look like I belonged. I carried house keys in a part of Los Angeles most people only imagine, held elevators, lit cigarettes, and unlocked doors. When the mistress came home, I washed the Porsche and filled it with gasoline. I made sure a particular brand of white wine stayed chilled, in endless supply.

I made runs to LAX. I became a sympathetic ear when given the signal, stayed invisible otherwise. Every morning, I retrieved the movie residual checks from the mailbox and deposited them. When asked, I drove friend-guests—pretty women and pretty men—around the city, for their game of musical beds. I watered plants, dusted glass knickknacks, wiped coke residue from the bathroom countertops, and sat beside the swimming pool, lifeguard to the inebriated.

When the frolic moved to tables in the hottest clubs on the strip, I nursed a vodka-and-milk and kept an eye on things from the end of the bar. I wasn't mean and I didn't have big muscles, but I had seen bad things and walked right on through. Maybe that stayed in my eyes. Even at twenty-one, I made people feel safe.

After a couple months, the endless blue days, the lush plantings and valet parking, the first-class comings and goings, the tequila glances and cocaine smiles, began to crack me at the edges. The sun grew hot and alien, illusive and painted-on. The palm trees got sinister. I have never known such emptiness, before or since.

People who get everything they want end up not wanting anything.

I had it made for a while. Then I got fired. I don't remember if there was a reason, and it doesn't matter. I took a bus a little way up the coast to a smaller city, went back to a punch clock and a cheap apartment across the street from Safeway. I budgeted the rent and ate the same lunch every day—two hot dogs, mustard only, with a large milk and the L.A Times sports page—at Ernie's Drive-in. I kept to myself, walked on the beach, and little by little the purple twilights and palm trees got romantic again.

Being canned from the best job I ever had saved my soul, but it made a near thing. Lost for good came too close for comfort.

So, I know a little about hell, too.

Someday, a Greyhound bus will drop me off at the entrance to the Askew. I'll find your footprints in the sand, Ghost, then follow them to where you wait. You'll be seated on a low cement wall, braiding pale flowers into your hair. The dogs at your feet will stir to look at me, then go back to sleep.

"You must be hungry from your trip," you'll say. "They serve grilled cheese here."

"Chicken noodle?" I'll ask.

Your smile takes my breath, says you were never gone.

"Naturally," you'll say. "Wouldn't be heaven, otherwise."

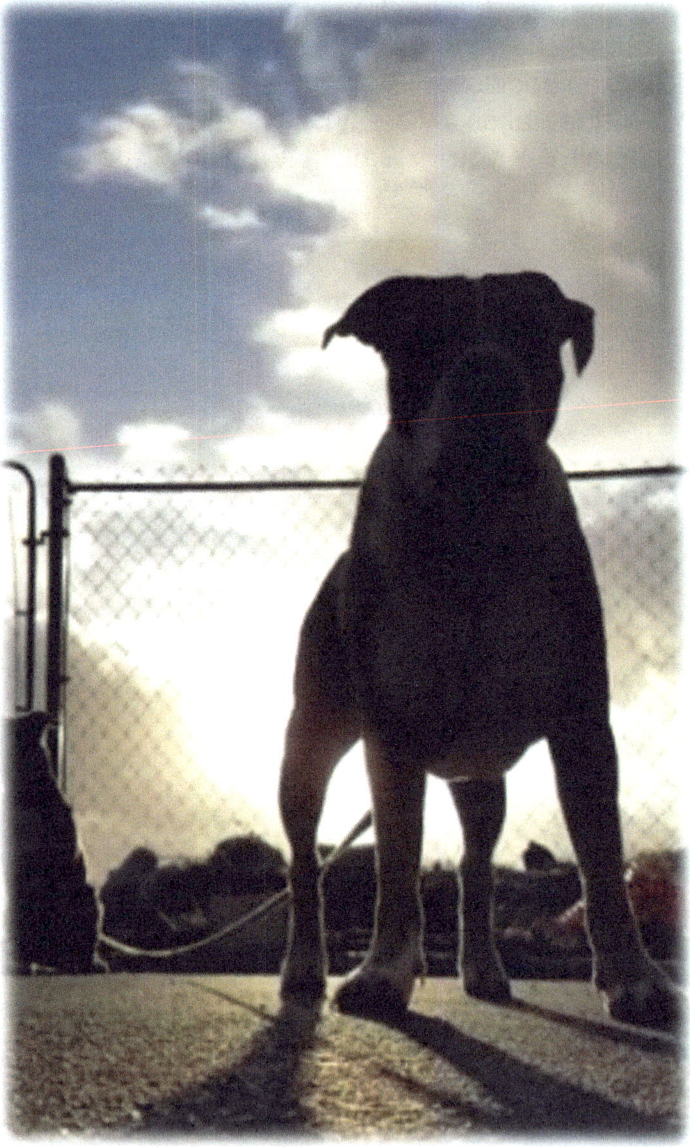

Love, Ghost

Dear Ghost,

    The rustle of palm fronds overhead always makes me sad. The smell of flowers never changes, so forever has to last forever. Good food tasted the same a hundred years ago. The shiver of falling in love, the hook of a private smile—they unfold exactly the same then and now. A first kiss—warm, moist, filled with sudden, unfamiliar fragrances—feels exactly the same as night wind on your face.
    None of that is an accident. There are no coincidences.
    I try to remember a time when I didn't feel you, Ghost, just out of sight. I can't.
    Summer of 1980: I'm riding an escalator up through the Eglinton Center in Toronto. The air-conditioning feels nearly cold, but hot streets glimmer at the top. I just turned out of the liquor store, so I have a paper-bagged fifth of lemon gin held in the crook of my left elbow.
    An enormous poster is mounted above the escalator. Supertramp released the album a year ago, but I still haven't bought it. The gleeful woman is a hundred-times life size. She holds a glass of orange juice aloft and leers at me. The crockery New York skyline floats behind her. I try to pick out Coney Island and can't. I've never been there.
    I'm young, but I know Atlantic beaches. I've swum the cotton-candy beautiful surf in Myrtle Beach. I know the Pacific, too. I was born there, so my heart never left. I've chased a beach ball in the cold waters off San Diego, walked the pier at Santa Monica. Later in my life, I'll walk the beaches in Santa Barbara, still oil-spattered by derricks that have been gone for decades. I'll paddle a Styrofoam board in the brown waters off Biloxi. I'll taste the

foam that washes onto Hampton beaches, as salty as everywhere else. The ocean doesn't care about rich.

I think I need to buy the album. I think I need to wade into the Atlantic at Coney Island. I have the sudden, strange notion that I'd start swimming and never stop. I'd paddle down to the Caribbean, through the Americas, past Baja and all the way to Hawaii.

I ride upward and look at breakfast in New York until the woman disappears overhead.

A pretty young woman, a day off, and a ferry boat ride to island beaches all wait for me at the top. She smiles down at me and motions me to hurry up, as if I can make the escalator go faster. I know she wears a bathing suit beneath her halter and shorts. I can't wait to see her with wet hair.

A hot summer day and Supertramp. For a while, I didn't think I needed anything else. Then I thought everything else—work, money, schedules, mortgages, car payments, appliances—mattered more. A lifetime later, I have the truth. I've put the gin away, but the hot streets, sweet smiles, days off, and a ferry boat rides to island beaches were the only things that mattered, the only things I'll bother to take with me when I go.

I've never did see the beach at Coney Island, though. At this point, I probably never will. It's late afternoon, and I have other places to go. Somehow, I'm glad I don't know that, on an escalator in 1979.

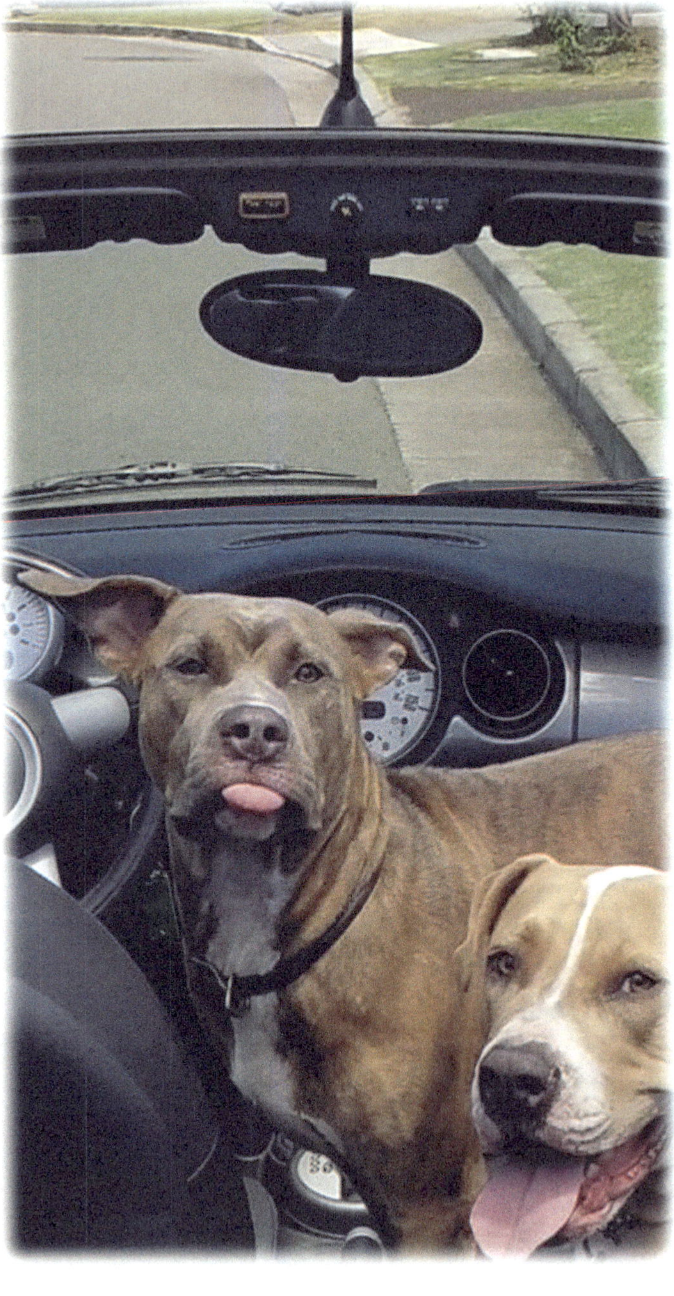

Love, Ghost

Dear Ghost,

I spot a Mercury Eight convertible tonight, parked a couple blocks from the beach. It sits beneath a streetlight, a wraith from the 1940s. Two-tone light over dark, I can't decide what color it really is, in the yellow light. I figure some proud owner has taken it out for its yearly run and will be along shortly, to roll it back into the garage, back under a nylon cover, back to sleep.

The dogs and I stop in the shadows, just in case. Then, and now.

You used to tell me we knew each other in a different place and time when we had other names. It seemed as unlikely and incomprehensible as a lot of what you said, but I had learned to listen. You persisted, casually reminding me of things I had no way to remember. You held my face in your hands and colored recollections crept in uninvited, asking to be tasted and smelled. I recalled standing with you on streets I had never seen. We went home together to an address where I never lived. On summer evenings, we listened to Billie Holiday on the radio and split a bowl of ice cream.

You thumbed hair behind your ear the way you did a long time ago, and you watched me to see if I recognized you. After a while, the idea of a different time together didn't seem crazy anymore.

I asked you what your name had been in that different life, playing along. You laughed like I teased you and never answered. I wish I had asked again. I have the idea it might make finding you easier, now. You never said your name, but you did tell me that your last car then had been a 1947 Mercury Eight convertible.

I had the strange notion you kept a bottle of Je Reviens on your dressing table in that other time, but you didn't much care for perfume. Same as now. Somehow, I knew you liked sandals. You undressed oranges in a single long peel, just like this time around. Your throat moved the same elegant way when you tipped a bottle back to drink. You tipped a dark glance my way. The long-ago you looked out at me.

Someday, I might remember your old name and write stories about you. If I do, maybe you'll find your way back. Gone, but not gone. I'll come back. *Je reviens.*

We loved dogs and hated mean people then, same as now. We liked popcorn, the ocean at night, and driving too fast with the top down. Perhaps I sat in a dark theater then, when the movie was over, to watch your credits roll, same as now.

"Don't die first," you said.

You didn't want to be left alone, so you asked me for the only thing I didn't want to give you. Maybe more than once. I wanted to stick fingers in my ears, but I loved you too much not to answer. It seemed an absurd request, because such a thing wasn't up to me, but you made me promise. Perhaps the universe listens when we cross our hearts and hope to die.

Now, the dogs wait with me on the edge of somebody's front lawn. We watch the empty sidewalk just in case a woman, the kind of slender that makes her look taller than she is, appears beneath the streetlights, silk-wrapped and barefoot, checking her purse for car keys. We stand quietly, until I get cold and they get restless. They're good dogs, but they aren't patient. They like to run to where they need to be.

"What year is this?" I ask them. "Right now."

If they know, they don't tell me.

I shake their leashes to take us on our way. Walking off, I don't look back. Maybe the Mercury convertible will sit outside all night. Maybe it was never there, the way we understand these things. On the other hand, maybe it's

been sitting in that same spot for the last eighty years or so.
   Gone, but not gone. *Je reviens.*

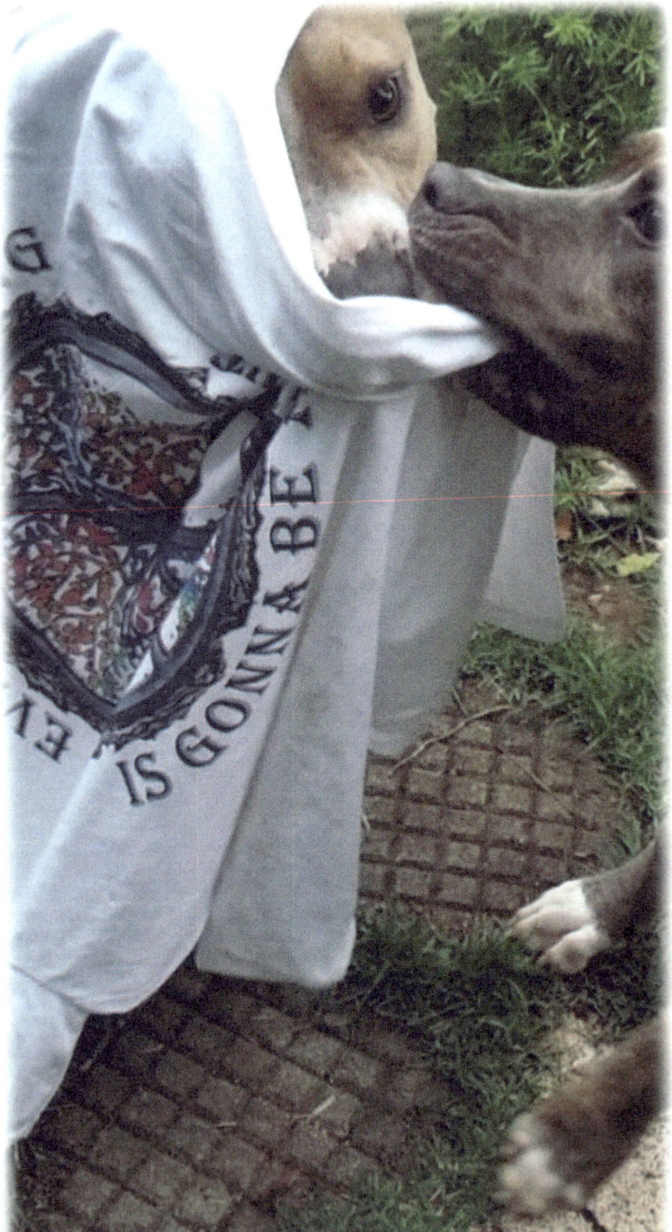
IS GONNA BE

Love, Ghost

Dear Ghost,

I wish it was always summer.

Home from swimming lessons, to sit at the kitchen table for a peanut butter lunch. My mom has her back turned at the counter. Plastic pitcher, packet of unsweetened Kool-Aid, aluminum crack of ice tray. One cube escapes, skitters across the linoleum floor. She swoops and yells at the dogs to leave it alone.

One-two sugar scoops from the bag, then stir with a wooden spoon. We don't get soda pop, because when you're all grown up you can drink whatever you like, but not here and not now. Not in this house.

Kool-Aid is the essence of American goodness, homemade with real sugar.

Cherry.

Forget about orange, strawberry, lemon-lime, raspberry, and grape. Summer is cherry, forever.

My mom notices the dogs are wet. They've found a place to swim. Nobody wonders where they've been—they have their own lives and it's none of our business. Hands full, she detours on her way to the table, holds the screen door open with a toe and yells for them to get out. They slink past her, three of them, brown and black and white. They'll be back for dinner. My dad feeds them in the garage.

Paper napkin and grape jelly. It's too hot for soup.

The window is open and the world outside drifts in. The smells are glorious—melting tar, honeysuckle, pool chlorine, and the electric ghosts of the thunderstorms coming tonight.

I'm going to the library after lunch. The Hardy Boys copy getting returned, *The Mystery of Cabin Island*, sits beneath my green baseball cap beside the front door. My mom yells not to forget my library card, like she always does, so I backtrack upstairs to my room to get it, like I always do. My Sting-Ray looks exactly like a motorcycle, (if someone dropped a motorcycle on the front sidewalk). Iodine and a band-aid on my right knee, and the scrape still stings a little when I swing my foot.

Pine Street to East Fifth to Main, bumping over curbs. In front of the library, I stand on the brake and leave a black mark on the sidewalk, just in case the little girl who sits at the front of my class happens to be passing by. Up the steps, touch the brass Andrew Carnegie letters, then into the dim smell of old paper.

"The Great Airport Mystery" is next. I never read out of order, but I take my time and look at the spines. *The Disappearing Floor, The Phantom Freighter, The Secret of Pirates' Hill.* All the good days yet to come. I'm going to climb a tree when I get home and have an hour to read before I start my paper route.

Dear Ghost, Whoever said Heaven is about harps and angels and choirs and clouds and hosannas never went there.

Heaven is July of 1967, a peanut butter and jelly small-town afternoon in Kansas.

One day, I'll go back. You'll be sitting at the counter in the drugstore, wearing fresh cotton and sandals, drinking from a straw. The bell over the door will jingle when I go in, and you'll pretend you don't recognize me. I'll pretend I don't recognize you, either.

You'll slide a cool glance my way and ask me if I believe in ghosts. Then you'll laugh your 1940s silver screen laugh. The beautiful sound of you will make me laugh, too.

"What are you drinking?" I'll ask.

You'll offer me the straw, and I'll remember the sweetness before I taste it. Cherry Kool-Aid means I'm home.

Bob Bickford

Bye for now.

Love, Ghost

Books by Bob Bickford

Dear Ghost
(Available in print, Kindle, audio)

Kahlo and Crowe Series

Girls in Pink
A Song for Chloe
Hau Tree Green
The Violet Crab
Deep Cherry Red
The Orange Groove
White Rabbit Hop

Other Novels

Deadly Kiss
Caves in the Rain
A Song for Chloe

A Blueberry Moon for Cora
(Available in print, Kindle, audio)

Amazon.com
and
BarnesandNoble.com

bobbickfordauthor.com
http://www.bobbickfordauthor.com/